DECLON 5

BY
David Dowson

www.daviddowson.com
www.daviddowson.co.uk

Table of Contents

Acknowledgments

Rachael and my mother, Beryl, who is always there for me, and my sister, Jan Webber, author of the Betty Illustrated children's books.

Also by David Dowson

- Chess for Beginners
- Chess for beginners Edition 2
- Into the Realm of chess Calculation
- Nursery Rhymes
- The Path of a Chess Amateur
- CHESS: the BEGINNERS GUIDE eBook:
- Dangers Within.

CHAPTER ONE DAVID SCARLET

David sat down on to his recliner chair that was on the porch,

From the porch, the his thoughts of leaving Carla alone, as he once done before, bore heavy upon his heart.

His actions had destroyed the very fabric of his loving union.

He felt trapped, tormented even, knowing he should be fulfilling his promise as a husband and lover against his obligations to his country.

He tried to identify cars that drove by to calm himself from the thoughts that troubled him. A lot was going on already in his life and more was about to go down, panicking would get him nowhere yet calming down seemed an impossible task now.

Since his long layoff from secret service activity, David had tried to live an everyday life, but it turns out normal is a far cry for an agent with so much experience and activity during his time in the service.

David had just returned from the hospital where he'd had his final check on his muscle spasm and (random speeches that had plagued him for a long time), his wife Carla was also admitted to the same hospital. David and Carla had been married a while but had a few miscarriages along the way, he wasn't taking too much of a chance this time around, he had taken her for checks and professional care when he found out she was pregnant.

He had a meeting with the director of the GCHQ and the Prime Minister in two days, his last mission as a spy before his deactivation had earned him significant respect in the espionage business. Since being reactivated a year ago, he had been reduced to desk jobs and missions without much focus. David knew more waited for him in the spy game and was patiently waiting for his great return

He was not expecting much, but he was excited when he was told he had a meeting with the Prime Minister. His closeness to the Prime Minister had given him an advisory role with the PM.

He would often visit Downing Street for council with the British leader and it was no surprise when the Prime Minister summoned him for a mission briefing.

David, still sitting on the porch, suddenly got up wanting one thing, not to leave Carla alone as he did once before, he was caught in thought wanting on one side to fulfil his duty to his country and his obligations to his wife. The last time he left his wife while she was pregnant, he lost a child and his wife. The effect of her attempt to take her own life had damaged her to the extent that they thought it'd be impossible for her to conceive; but here they were, against all odds, she was pregnant, he wasn't sure what to do but he needed to find out what the mission was and that would determine his response.

That evening, David left his home to see his wife at the hospital, he walked through Downing Street as he beheld the magnificence of the spectacle that housed several British dignitaries. He was going to make a stop at the shopping mall to pick up some things that Carla had demanded.

The walk down Downing Street was much needed to help him clear his head, people flocked the often-busy pathways. He had often wondered why Downing Street, the residence of one of, if not the most important persons in all of Europe, was so accessible. He walked through as he wondered what his mission with the Prime Minister was about. David did not give much thought to the meeting but to his wife Carla who lay sick in a hospital bed. He entered Larimer Square, a few metres away from Downing Square. A spectacle that caught his eyes despite the times he had been there, the children running round gave it a sense of peace and delight, he walked in wanting to pick up the cake and ice cream that Carla had asked for. The thought that he was going to be a father gave him a feeling of joy, it was a new feeling and one he was willing to embrace. Carla was his first love, and nothing would give him more joy than spending the rest of his life with her and raising their child . He walked into Larimer Square wanting to get what he came for and go to his wife. A man dressed in a hoodie and wearing shades stood in one corner. David tried not to think too much of it as the man looked like he was talking to someone, but his spy instincts did not allow him. The man looked suspicious but not enough to confront him. He walked into the creamery to get his order when he heard screams, he rushed out and saw the same man armed with an AKM rifle. The man wasn't alone, there were five others, dressed similarly and armed with automatic rifles. Those were the ones he could see, he needed to be sure that was all of them. He snuck back into the creamery and hid himself behind a freezer to avoid being noticed. He had to do something about the situation, he wasn't as young as he used to be, but David had a strong physique, trying his best possible to stay in shape for whenever the service would need him. This was not how he planned to spend his day, but he had to do something about it. This was a hostage situation and the shopping mall had been sealed off from the outside world, he had to stop this from the inside. His intention wasn't to stop it in style like James Bond, his move was to stop it just like David Scarlett would. He was a super-spy now and he had to live up to the billing. David slowly sneaked out from behind the freezer after the sounds of the hostage-takers had faded. He walked out of the ice cream shop as quietly as he could and moved into a store that sold mobile devices next door, trying to contact the outside world. They had a signal jammer, separating the shopping mall from the outside world, making it impossible to contact the police or anyone else for that matter. His task had become difficult, he had to sort the situation from within.

To be sure of the total number of men there, he had to go straight to the camera room to get full footage of the entire shopping mall. again, The screening room was on the other wing, he had to cut through the entire lobby to get there which meant cutting through the kidnappers. It was not going to be an easy task, but he had to do it, nonetheless.

Edged —

CHAPTER TWO: HOSTAGE RESCUE

Locked from contacting the Police, David knew the task of saving everyone in the mall would prove difficult and there might come a time when he'd need to choose between himself and the hostages.

But he knew first-hand the choice to make. He had placed the lives of the people of Britain over a handful of times and he was not afraid to do it yet again. The implication this time was worse than the times he had been in the situation.

David headed out of the shop and through the hallway, exercising as much care as he was in a stealth mission. This was not exactly the mission, but it was a chance to show the service that he had what it took to accept high-profile missions. Halfway through the hallway, he looked outside and saw a handful of police officer parked outside trying to find a way into the shopping mall. He knew what he had to do, and he had to communicate with them somehow. If he could get through to the police officers, he could create a plan to free the hostages and end the situation.

Halfway through the hallway on the second floor, and the hostages down in the lobby, the plan was not to get caught so he could pinpoint the location of all the hostage-takers. He saw a child, a young girl, who had her hands over her mouth as she sobbed, and a woman lying down in a pool of blood, it was her mother. He knew getting to the screening room was secondary, he had to protect the child from the assailants before making his way.

He placed his index finger across both of his lips and crawled across the hallway. He was close to the child when the mannequin she was hiding behind fell to the ground. The shopping mall overrun by fear was as quiet as a cemetery, the only sounds heard were those of the assailants threatening the hostages. The silence was broken by the loud thud of the mannequin hitting the shop floor echoing all through the shopping mall, the attention of everyone, the hostages and the kidnappers was drawn to the sound.

His cover had been blown, he had to hide and hide the child as well before they got to him, he tried to make no sounds as he heard the words, "You, go check it out, make sure you get to the bottom of .he did, he was outnumbered and couldn't risk a shootout with them. The element of surprise was what he had, and he needed to make good use of it.

 He pulled the child into a toy shop, it had an open space with so many toys, some big enough to fit a human child and others so small they could fit in the pocket of a human child.
He placed the child between two huge dolls as he hid himself in a pile of clothes, he had pleaded with the child to remain completely still to ensure they were not discovered.
The man climbed the floor, walking along the hallway, not sure if there was anybody on the premises. He was careful not to make a wrong step and get caught unawares, but he did not find anyone.

The man looked down the railings, "There is no one here boss, it is empty," he said in heavily accented English. His voice awakened tones of memories in David, he was Russian. This reminded David of the times he spent in Tver trying to rescue his comrades and go back home with information. That the man was Russian made David even angrier. What are the Russians doing here? I hope this is not going to lead to an international incident with Russians taking English citizens as hostages in the UK.

Russians taking English civilians as hostages in Britain wasn't accepted, he had to take them down one after the other. The boss who was in the lobby looked up at the one on the same floor as David. "You heard the sound, didn't you? Things do not just fall on their own Yuri, something or someone made them fall, find me that something or someone and bring them to me dead or alive else I will have your head on a plate."

Yuri, murmuring as he took his hand off the railings, looked around and saw the mannequin, the only item on the floor. He walked close to it, looked around but saw nothing. Whatever caused it to fall must have headed here, he thought as he walked into the toy shop, he tiptoed to not alert whoever was in the shop. He passed David, who went unnoticed. He was searching when he heard sounds, he followed the sounds and found himself staring right at the child

He looked at the child and picked her up from her hiding spot, "So you are the little damsel in distress, aren't you just precious," he said to her. He turned to make his way out of the store. David grappled him in a sleeper hold, his right-hand firm around Yuri's throat, and the other pushing his head hard against his right arm, reducing the air in his lungs. Yuri struggled to stay awake but could not hold on for long, he fainted.

One down. David stretched his hand for the child to take hold. Saving the child felt good, but he could not keep her with him, her presence was going to slow him down.

He carried the child carefully out of the toy shop, both bent to prevent being seen by the hostage-takers down in the lobby. If Yuri didn't come back soon, the rest would come searching for him, and once they'd found him, they'd know there was someone in the shopping mall working against them.

He gave up on trying to find out how many they were and focused on plucking them down one after the other, it did not matter their numbers. If he could take them out significantly, it'd give the hostages time to escape or give the police officers time to think of a plan. He took her to a fashion hub and tucked her carefully into a pile of clothes.

He looked at her, she looked like,
he was going to cry, "Hey, you haven't even told me your name, I am David, what's yours?" name
She smiled, "I am Kim."
"Hey Kim, I need you to wait for me,
I'm going to punish those bad men and then I'll come back for you, and I'll take you for
ice cream."
The child jumped with joy, excited at the prospect of ice cream, "Promise David?" she said.

Promising someone yet again for situations that were beyond his control, this whole scenario was taking David down memory lane, it wasn't the first time he had promised someone when he wasn't sure of the outcome, but he didn't care, "I promise, now just stay quiet and don't move." He left the child to find a better spot where he could see all the kidnappers prop

CHAPTER THREE: ONE BY ONE

David left for the screening room, not bothered about numbers but positions, he didn't want to be taken by surprise. He had himself glued to the wall, stealthily walking through the hallway when he heard voices, it was the leader of the gang, "Yow, Yuri, what are you doing there? I sent you to do one thing and you can't, why do I pay you so much when all you bring is incompetence? Yuri! Yuri! That bastard has left the task I gave him.

Markov, you go look for him, knock some sense into him before you come back."

David knew that Markov couldn't find Yuri where he had kept him, the success of his stealth operation depended on surprise, he had to ensure that no one found the bodies that he had disposed of. He sneaked back into the shop where he had stashed Yuri's body, he hid behind the entrance door, and Markov went straight in, they had seen Yuri go in and knew where they saw him last. Markov walked in, careful as well, he went into the storeroom, David was behind him. David lunged to give him a sleeper hold but Markov countered, smacking David's hands away from his neck.

Markov now had his eyes on David, he brought out a knife from his belt, ready to strike. Markov, huge and firm, slashed with his knife held firmly in his right hand. David avoided the knife only to be received by a well-dealt blow from Markov's left fist, the blow made a crisp contact with David's lower lips, causing blood to spill on the floor. David staggered, refusing to allow himself the deck.

Markov threw a swift kick at David, who tried to avoid it but was met with Markov's left fist yet again. David couldn't avoid this one but protected himself with his left hand. It wasn't much of a defence as he felt the full force of Markov's blow, it felt to him like he had fractured something as he struggled to lift his hand after the punch.

David couldn't let Markov dictate the pace of the fight, Markov taunted him on the floor when David landed a blow on Markov's crotch, sending the huge Russian to the ground. David kicked his head as hard as he could, knocking Markov out. He tied Markov up and pulled him into the same room he had kept Yuri. Two down and more to go.

He knew the five men he had seen at the lobby couldn't be all of them, he had taken out two and there were three left.

There could be more elsewhere, and if they had taken charge of the camera room, they'd notice him. He had to get there soon but he also needed to secure the ones he had knocked out. He left the room, heading straight for the camera room, he sneaked past doors, avoiding being in the line of sight of the camera. It was smooth sailing, getting to the camera door, he pushed the door open as quietly as he could and found two men strapped in duct tape. He turned around and saw a woman, she had a handgun pointed at his face.

"You don't look like one of them Russians, who are you and what are you looking for?"

David, with his hand in the air, explained, "The name's David Scarlett, I'm certainly no Russian, I'm an Englishman who happened to be in the shopping mall at the same time it was hijacked by a band of Russians. I'm out here trying to find a way out for us all." She looked at him. He wasn't among them; she had seen the footage of him take two of them down, but she just wanted to be sure.

She dropped her gun, looked at him closely, "Hi, I'm Sarah Croft, like you, I was at the shopping mall for a little shopping and met this scumbag trying to jack the place."

David was happy to see someone who hadn't been taken hostage and wasn't among the attackers. "I reckon you took these two lads out, yeah?" She nodded her head positively to suggest she had defeated two Russian goons all by herself. "How did you do it without any help?" She smiled gently; it was a much-needed relief in a situation that was starting to blow out of proportion.

She looked at him as she responded, "I am ex Special Forces, tactical warfare, I have a little training on hand-to-hand combat."

David, apprehensive, walked away from her, "A little you say? This sure looks like a lot, remind me never to get on your bad side, Sarah." The pair laughed quietly as David headed for the screens. He had it in his sights, he could tell their overall numbers once and for all, and with Sarah on his side, they could inflict significant damage on the gang.

Sarah looked at David, "You look like a lad with a decent head on his shoulders? What's your plan? You do have one, yeah?"

"I haven't thought of any concrete plan, but one thing I do know is that we can't take them head-on, we have just a gun and it's a handgun, they have automatic rifles, it's going to leave us really handicapped. We have to take them out silently, also we have to communicate with the police officers somehow, and I know now that the security room is safe, I need you to head on to the top of the shopping mall and try to alert the police. I am going to go back into the lobby and attend to them again. I reckon the plan isn't that difficult?"

She shook her head as if to suggest it wasn't, she continued, "I only just met you, but I like how you think. Be safe, I'll see you outside."

David left the camera room and back into the shopping mall, he needed to free the hostages. Leaving people in danger wasn't

his modus operandi. He was close to the lobby when he heard footsteps, the absence of Markov and Yuri had taken more time than expected, there were just three now and he could take them quietly if he made the effort. He snuck behind a big flower arrangement allowing two of them to pass without noticing him. He had collected the handgun from Sarah, and he could shoot this time. He had them cornered and this was where he wanted to be.

They passed David, he came out slowly, pointing the gun at them, he shouted, "Hey bastards, I'm not in the business of killing people today but I need you both to put down your weapons and make this a lot easier for all of us. I wouldn't want to splatter your brain matter everywhere, but I would do it without hesitation if you don't do what I ask. I'm not too cheerful today so you best be doing what I say if you wish to see beyond this day." The men dropped their guns, carried their hands in the air as he approached them. wasn't going to take any chances, he hit one of them so hard with the barrel of the gun that he stumbled to the ground. He had lost his element of surprise, the other one jumped him before he could gather himself, both of them rolling down the stairs, they weren't out in the lobby yet but the boss had noticed the ruckus. He had his rifle in his arm and opened fire towards the direction of the fighting, David took cover on the railings, bullets raining like fire and brimstone on the shopping mall walls. The gunshots rumbled through the air as the coppers outside took cover thinking they were being shot at. The hostages covered their ears as the silence in the shopping mall allowed the gunshots to sound as if connected to speakers.

OSU had already made its way to the entrance of the shopping mall wanting to come in, David had reduced the number of attackers inside but he didn't think they wouldn't account for OSU intervention, they must have done something to prevent them from coming in, the boss had a bag fitted close to his feet, it didn't look to David like the men came here with the intention of collecting a ransom and leaving alive. The bag was filled with ammunition, it looked like they came here to make a statement, and the ease with which the boss rained bullets in his direction showed they were very prepared to do just that.

David covered his ears as the shooting continued, it was so rampant that the boss had hit his compatriot multiple times but that didn't stop him. OSU had seen Sarah on the roof and tried to enter the shopping mall. They rammed one of the doors behind to gain access. David wasn't aware of their entrance and focused on saving the hostages. He heard an explosion, the tremor rocked the building, sending debris to the ground. David tumbled down, and the boss, unbalanced, staggered, unable to maintain his position.

The boss regained control, laughing, "You fools think I will allow you to come in so easily, I have laced all entrances with C4, the more you try to come in, the more you put the people in here at risk. The building will fall from its foundations, and we'll all die. Look at me Englishman, do I look like I came here with the intention of leaving? I came here to die for a just cause,"

"What cause is that? Who sent you to put innocent lives in danger?"

The boss laughed, "Soon you will find out, soon all of Britain will find out, soon the entire world will find out who we are and then it will be the right time, it will be the right time to make our mark on the world."

He had his rifle in his hand, the ruckus had given him the opportunity to change his cartridge. He walked slowly towards David, who tried to find an opening to shoot, but whenever he did, the boss shot back. David had a shopping mall chance when the boss' phone rang. He took cover to receive the short call and came out of hiding with his hand stretched out, his gun on the floor. He screamed, "ISIS FOREVER." He exploded right in front of everybody, his body parts flying all over the place like birds on an open city square. The explosion was simultaneous, all seven hostage-takers had done the same thing.

The suicide explosion wasn't enough to harm the hostages who were a bit far away from the terrorist, but it sent David flying a few meters into the air, he bumped his head against the wall and fell unconscious. The ruckus had calmed down, hostages ran around the place trying to find safety, and David lay still on the floor like he was dead. Sarah, coming down from the rooftop, found him lying motionless. She tried her hardest to pull him up, but there were still explosives laced around the building exits and entrances. Sarah tried to regain his consciousness, but he was out cold.

Another explosion rocked the building, David slowly opened his eyes, the world spinning in circles as he tried to regain full consciousness. He slid up and rested his back on the wall. He looked up and saw Sarah, he shouted, "Don't let them go out, the doors are packed with explosives to go up when you open them. I also think the building is laced with timer explosives as well. It is supposed to go off, they didn't take these people hostage for ransom, they took them for death."

Sarah, unsure why someone would do something so wrong, asked him, "Did they say who they were? And how do we get out of here before the explosives go out?"

David struggled to pull himself up, "They did but now is not the time, the only way out is in the back, I heard one of the explosives go off. A OSU team tried to force their way in and that caused an explosion. They must have set one off, and it means, to get out of here, we have to make use of the entrance they had created. Try to calm the people down, I'll head out back and see if the path is free of explosives."

Sarah looked at him with so much admiration, "For one who's not a cop, you really are good at it, and you really treat people like they are family, stay safe this time, I shouldn't wish to find you unconscious yet again." David smiled and nodded as he left for the back of the building while Sarah tried to calm the hostages down. She shouted at them, "everyone, you can't make it through the doors. The doors have been packed with explosives, going through them would mean sudden death. You don't have to worry though; I have someone trying to find a way out for us. The coppers outside are trying to find a way for you all to go out with, just stay still, we have this under absolute control."

David ran through the shopping mall, hurt but eager to save, he made way for the explosion that had rocked the building prior, the blast wasn't a joke, it had so much force that a significant part of the shopping mall had crumbled. The opening he expected wasn't there, the debris had covered the passage. He knew the doors were packed with explosives and they were timer explosives set at strategic positions in the shopping mall. He had a serious dilemma, he couldn't force the hostages through the door, and he couldn't leave them in the shopping mall for long, it might come down. He also didn't have enough time to locate the explosives to deactivate them, he didn't know how many there were, even if he were to deactivate them with Sarah's help.

CHAPTER FOUR: EVACUATION

David didn't know how but he had to evacuate the hostages, the only exit or entrance that wasn't compromised was the rooftop. He ran to the camera room, found phones lying idle, picked one up and put a call through to the coppers. The signal jammers had been disabled, he dialled 112 and there was a response almost immediately, "This is the metropolitan police, what is your emergency?"

"This is David Scarlet with the GCHQ, I'm stuck in the Larimer, I have found a way to put the terrorists out of commission, but the hostages can't exit the building. The doors have been packed with explosives and there is a timer bomb somewhere in the building. I don't think I can locate the bomb right now under the circumstances, so I have to evacuate the hostages as soon as possible."

"I will direct you to the anti-terrorism squad, they will give you all the assistance you need. Thank you, David, for your assistance."

He waited a few seconds and someone else responded, "David, this is Captain David James of the metropolitan police anti-terrorism squad, what is your situation?" David grew impatient, he had told the lady that received the call initially, he had no time to say it again but delaying the information anymore would put the hostages in even more risk.

"There's no way out for us at the moment, the doors are packed with explosives and there is a bomb somewhere in the building which would go off in a time I'm not certain, we have to find a way to evacuate immediately. I have a plan, but I don't know how feasible it will be."

The captain was willing to take whatever chance there was, "Speak up David, whatever it is you want, we will do it, we have no other option."

"It has to be a rooftop evacuation captain, the doors are going to explode if we open them, there are no other entrances or exits. The only door that won't explode is the rooftop door, my guess is their plan was to demand a helicopter to escape via the roof top but for some sick reason, they took their own lives still in the shopping mall. I suggest we get a chopper here, evacuate the hostages before it's too late. I don't know how long the bomb will count but I expect that before I go back in to bring the hostages, a chopper will be waiting for us."

The captain went quiet, "I don't think a chopper can be ready that quickly, we have to put a call through to air command and it'll take it a little while to get here David."

Disappointed, David was about to drop the phone when he had an idea, "Are there news choppers out there?" The captain responded positively, David continued, "I don't know how many you've got out there but please, while air command readies a chopper to pick the rest of them, we need you to get those news choppers to pick the hostages. I know this is unconventional but it's the option we have. I can't stand still and watch them die, well I won't because I'd be dead myself. Please, captain, make this work."

"Ok David, I will, do me a favour and usher the hostages to the rooftop, the available choppers will convey as much as it can before air command sends us one. Thanks man, I hope to see you outside."

David left the security room, heading straight for the lobby to inform Sarah he had established communications with the Police officers and that the hostages should go to the rooftop. As he ran, the opposite wing of the shopping mall, where the hostages were, exploded. He was close to the explosion as it rocked the building, the blast sent David flying meters from where he was, debris falling from the roof of the shopping mall into the lobby threatening the safety of the hostages. He tried to get up but felt a sharp pain shoot through his left leg, he looked at it and saw a rod piercing through his thighs, the pain was unbearable as he screamed his lungs out attracting the attention of Sarah, who stood at the lobby awaiting his signal.

David stood up, standing by the rails, he was in pain but couldn't stay still else he'd die and wouldn't see his wife and unborn child. He limped to the rails where he saw Sarah, looking in his direction, "David, what's next?"

Still limping, he shouted back, "Take everybody to the roof, there are choppers waiting to evacuate them all, I'll be right behind you." The building was coming down as debris fell all over the place, it wasn't going to hold on for long, he had to be sure everyone was safe and fast.

He was limping away when he heard a cry, it was the voice of a child from a store behind, it was Kim. He had left her there for safety but the entrance into the store was compromised, it was coming down. He would have to carry the child out if she couldn't run by herself. The odds were stacked against him, but he had to save her, he couldn't leave her behind, he had given her his word and he sure as hell was going to keep his promise.

As the hostages made for the stairs, Sarah looked back to thank David for his efforts, but he was nowhere to be seen, she called out his name but there was no reply. She couldn't leave him behind, she went back, screaming his name as she searched everywhere for him. David limped into the store where he had left Kim, the integrity of the store already compromised, he didn't have full power as his right leg was bleeding, and he tied the injury with a cloth he found on the floor to keep pressure on it.

He had Kim in his arms, the building coming down on both of them, he struggled to navigate through the debris with more falling on the way, making his movements even harder. He was just by the door when another bomb exploded, this time affecting the foundations of the building. Cracks moved up the wall of the section he was in, it felt like that wing would fall off the entire building. David could barely run, his leg bleeding more now, he was starting to lose energy as he was losing blood.

Kim's weight wasn't exactly easy to carry in the current circumstances, he was already giving up, the explosion rocked yet again, with more debris falling off the roof, falling just beside David and Kim. He was already slipping with the part of the building breaking off when he saw Sarah, she stood just across the cracks, her hands stretching forward as she gestured to David to strive further to hand her the child. He took Kim from off his bosom, he dropped her gently, gesturing for her to walk to Sarah, the child hesitated but he insisted. Kim, with tears on her eyes, shouted as Sarah held her firmly, "I'm waiting outside."

David, looking at the child, knew in his heart that he had to make it, not just for Kim but for Carla, his unborn child and his mission to Britain. He held on for dear life to a pillar that stood in front of him, he made his way gently for the door, Sarah couldn't leave him behind, she stood there trying to wait for him to make a move. He tussled with the building already crooked, her hands stretched as she held on to the rail behind her, she had dropped Kim as she made efforts to save David. Kim, not willing to let David die, held on Sarah's legs with one hand as she held on to the rail with the other.

Seeing the resolve of the child to save his life, David had more to live for, he pulled himself off the pillar as he stretched his hand to grab hold of Sarah. He struggled as he grunted with every movement, the pains from the injury in his legs struck hard like a batter for a pro baseball team, the more he tried to move, the more he could feel blood leaking from the injury. He had hit his head earlier and he was barely alive. It was his adrenaline that spurred him on, but whatever it was, it was an ardent desire to survive. David held on to Sarah like a beast holding on to prey after having no meal for weeks, he wouldn't let go. Kim screamed as though she was the one preventing him from falling.

Sarah mustered all the power she could as she placed her legs against the wall to allow her enough force to pull David up. He made the work easier for her as he pulled himself up as well, he crossed the door when a significant part of the room collapsed into the floor. He fell on Sarah, Kim lying down just beside them. Sarah looked at him with relief in her eyes, "You promised you'd be fine, that didn't look very fine to me."

He looked at her and smiled, "I had it all under control, you didn't need to help."

The pair laughed as they ran down the hallway, making their way towards the stairs. The blades of choppers just beyond sounded as they headed for the rooftop. The hostages had been evacuated completely by the time they got there; the chopper was about to leave. David screamed as loud as his lungs could carry him, Sarah on one side pulling him as he laid on her shoulders and Kim on the other side as she made an attempt to lift his already wounded right leg. The chopper was about to fly away when it saw them. It was the metropolitan police's hummingbird chopper, a forty-person capacity bird. The wings spanning nine feet each, spinning generating winds that could blow a child away.

The rescue team members rushed down from the chopper to help David up as he almost fell to the ground, they picked him up and helped him into the bird. The bird had just left the ground when the main explosion rocked the building. The vibrations so strong that it shattered glass in nearby buildings, the sound like a nuclear warhead had made contact with earth, there was a bright light that swept the entire perimeter before a thunderous sound followed. The building collapsed layer by layer into the ground.

David looked at the shopping mall as it fell into the ground, he let out a smile as he faded into utter darkness. Sarah called out his name, but he had lost too much blood and was too weak to respond.

CHAPTER FIVE:
RECOVERY

"David, David?"

David struggled to get up from the pitch-black darkness. He felt hands touch his skin repeatedly, but he couldn't respond as quickly as he would have liked. The constant movement, the feel of latex on his skin, the smell of drugs, he was in a hospital, but for how long had he been there?

He strained to open his eye lids and he saw Sarah Croft, his special agent sidekick that had helped him overcome those terrorists. He looked right next to her, and he saw Mark and Laura, Carla's parents with Laura clutching his fist not wanting to let go even for a second.

David understood why Mark and Laura were there, but Sarah, it made no sense to him. He could see Sarah for whom she was, she was a lean woman, about five inches plus tall and short brown hair. For someone who was Special Forces and subject to training, she looked quite pleasant to the eyes or at least that was what he thought.

Laura was the most worried of all three visitors that stood by David, he was injured and still in obvious pains, but his only concern was finding out how his wife was fairing, "How's Carla? I reckon she is fine and haven't found out of my escapades at Larimer?"

Mark was quick to respond, "Let Carla be Carla for the time being and focus on getting better. You have a history of getting hurt." His voice wasn't steady as was his look, bothered that David came face to face with death but didn't want his worries made obvious as that would throw Laura into a frenzy and probably affect Carla.

David tried to sit up, and for every move he made, he grunted in pain. He had accumulated more injuries in a day than he had his entire career in the service. He reached for his thighs and saw that his legs had been bandaged. He felt discomfort in his head, where he also had bandages. He must have sustained more injuries than he feared.

He placed his hands on his legs, "What is the nature of my injuries? Has the doctor mentioned?"

Mark replied, "Broken ribs, torn muscles, fractured skull. It looks like you'll be here a while." David, uncomfortable with the prospect of staying in a hospital longer than he expected, tried to pull himself up.

Laura rushed to his side, restraining his movements, "You are not leaving here anytime soon, you are going to stay and heal and be fine for Carla, she needs you at this time in her life. You shouldn't make any rash decision if you care about her.

"I was surprised when I saw the incident in the news, I didn't know you were in the shopping mall at the time as well, good thing Carla was asleep at the time. I have been following the news of the hostage taking at Larimer Square, I had no idea you were there. I have to say that when I tried contacting you a couple of times and couldn't, I started to panic. Thank God, you made it out alive. There were lots of people here who wanted to see you just before you woke up."

David adjusted to sit up properly, he was in obvious pains, "Did everybody make it out alive?" He looked at Sarah, expecting her to respond to that question because she was the only one who could have an answer to that question.

Sarah answered, "The police were still trying to account for everyone in the shopping mall when I left them. The news account had it that a civilian life was lost and that seven terrorists self-detonated, bringing the total death to eight. I guess the dead civilian was the baby's mother, Kim, the one you risked your life to save."

David looked at Sarah yet again, he wasn't done quizzing her, "What did the news report say about the attack, any terrorist group claiming responsibility? Have they found out who orchestrated an attack on a part of London that had more children than it does adults?"

Sarah kept her head down, "No, no group has claimed responsibility, but the police and other bodies have been investigating to ensure that they get to the bottom of the whole attack."

David looked at Mark, Laura and Sarah, he had questions for all of them, but he didn't feel he should talk more, for every word uttered, his entire body ached like he had been beaten by a crowd, but the questions were necessary, he asked Sarah, "What of Kim? Where is she?"

Sarah looked at him sadly, "Well her mother was killed during the attack, efforts to find her father have proved abortive. The police are doing all they can but if they can't get to him, I guess she will be taken by social services and a perfect family would find her and raise her. She's still a baby and has her entire life in front of her."

He didn't like the idea of leaving her out there alone, he said to Laura, "If her father isn't contacted, I'd like to have her. I know Carla is pregnant and I'm super happy for her, for us but I felt a connection with this child, I mean she risked her precious little life for me, I want her to grow up with me if her father isn't found."

Laura, not sure why but understanding the attachment he must have developed for the child when faced with a near-death experience, accepted it, "You can adopt this Kim if social services can't find her father, but you'd have to talk to Carla about it and that would be when you are feeling a lot better so rest up for now."

David agreed to Laura's terms as he laid down on the bed, he was going to rest but he stopped, sat up again and demanded one last thing, "Is there any way I could see Kim, I don't know if it's because Carla's expecting but I felt a connection with the child, she spoke to me like she had always known me, she was willing to risk her life for mine. She lost her mom, I lost mine some months ago, but I still feel the pain like it just happened. I know she's a child and she'd forget it in no distant time, but I wish I could see her before I rest, please. "Laura was going to refuse as she didn't see the ne ed, but Sarah agreed, "I'll fetch her for you and you'll have all the time you need to see her, you deserve it but don't get too used to it yet. Stay patient, yours is on its way but if you must get used to this child, I can't stop you." Sarah walked away from the room to plan for Kim to be brought to David. Laura and

Mark walked out when David stopped them, "Laura, Mark, how long was I out?"Mark walked up to him, patted him on the shoulder, "You have been out a few days. I just want to let you know that we are happy that you are fine. Rest up now son, your friend will see to your request, we just want you to be fine. Promise you'll rest?"

David placed his hand on Mark's as he gestured for Laura to hold his fist, he felt so much love with his wife's family like they were his from birth, he said to them both passionately, "I will be fine. Thank you for all you do for me and for Carla. I love you both a great deal." He let them go as they headed for the exit. David tried to rest; his mind unable to stay still. Images of his parents trying to recreate the accident that claimed their lives ran through his head. He thought of Carla as she laid in the hospital bed or with her parents at home. He wondered what the Prime Minister and the Director of the GCHQ, had to brief him. He considered the fate of Kim, he had to keep her, he had to watch her grow if no one else took her in.

He stayed there alone with his thoughts, his eye glanced through the room, he had balloons and flowers laced all over the place. He saw cards on the table, a lot of them, some of the balloons had the description, "A true hero," inscribed on them, saving lives had become a norm for him and it was what he did while in active service. He picked up the cards and began to read through them, he saw so many touching messages but none more precious to him than the card that was sent to him by Kim. She wrote it with a fondness for him, it read, "To the bravest man I have ever met, you are my hero and I am here waiting for you to leave the hospital so we can have ice cream together."

He smiled as he held her card so close to his chest, there was no reason but he cherished the child. He had her card the whole time as his mind travelled towards a beautiful picture of himself, Carla and a child having a picnic together, his mind was playing tricks on him, it was presenting a picture of his desires right before his eyes. He had always believed that seeing things before they happen have a way of preventing them from happening.

He had been alone almost an hour and as he tried to sleep, he heard a voice so sharp that it pierced him even deeper than a bullet would. A surge of joy passed through his entire body as he looked at the door and standing before him was Sarah and Kim. The child rushed over to him, climbing his bed and jumping on his broken body, he was in pain but tried not to show it so she wouldn't stop the joy that she had brought to his hospital space.

She looked at him straight into his eyes, the joy that radiated around her was contagious, for someone who had no family, Kim had so much joy within her. She was only a child, but she had the attitude needed to go through life's hardest situations. "I have been here a lot of times but you have been sleeping. You are a baby that sleeps so long. I thought you weren't going to wake up like my mommy."

David, careful not to say the wrong things said to her, "I'm going to be here for you. I'm not going anywhere. I know you miss your mommy, but I promise everything will be fine. When I get out of the hospital, I am going to come over to where you are now and take you home with me." Kim liked the idea of staying with David.

The pair spent hours talking to each other about every and any little thing with Sarah seared waiting for them to finish when they felt like so he could take Kim home. The pair had played games so much that Kim was already tired and fell asleep in David's arms. David looked at Sarah who had a smile on her face as she stared at them, "Is there something you want to say?"

Sarah stood up from the chair to pick the child up, "She adores you and you have a soft spot for her, I don't know why you do but you do. She's fragile now, you shouldn't be making promises to her, you are the one person she has identified that can protect her and be her friend. You haven't spoken to your wife about her, it's not safe giving her the impression that you'll take her with you when your wife hasn't given her say so. I'm not saying what you have with her isn't good, but every girl needs a father figure in their life and without hers, she has identified you as hers, I hope you will be there for her as you are promising her."

David looked at the child as she slept peacefully on his body, he didn't know why but he wanted her in his life, he looked back at Sarah, "I will make her life easier; I will be her father and all she wants from me, I have identified her as well as my child. She has a free spirit and a loving personality, and I don't want her to lose that because she lost her parents. I will give her all the love she needs."

Sarah smiled, sat down, and rested her head on the back ear of the chair, "I should allow her sleep some more on her father's chest." David liked the feel of being a father, he smiled as he eventually fell asleep.

CHAPTER SIX: ENQUIRY

As David, Kim and Sarah slept, he felt like he was at peace. David woke up to the sound of voices, whispers, he struggled to open his eye lids. He opened his eyes and saw that the room was alive, more alive than it was when he fell asleep. There were four heavily built men, dressed in suits in the room, two standing on each side of his bed, he didn't know who they were so he held Kim closely, not willing to give her back to anyone.

One on his right-hand side spoke up, "I am Special Agent Jack Daniels, this is Callum Chambers, Donny Pratt and Hughes

Higginbottom, and we are with the MI6." David wondered in his heart what they wanted to do with him, he could tell they were the secret service when they walked in as there was nothing secret about them. Their blazer suits always gave them away but for some reason, they never stopped wearing them.

Jack started speaking, "When reports of the terrorists attack you stopped reached the office of the MI6, we knew we had to speak with you."

David slowly sat up as the conversation was towing a line he was all too familiar with. Jack continued, "We just wanted to know, did they say anything that stood out while you were there?" David looked up at the ceiling like he was trying to remember what he heard in the shopping mall.

He spoke back, "The events are a little fuzzy, but the leader said something about us finding out who they were soon, the work will soon know who they were and shouted *ISIS Forever* before he blew himself up." Sarah had opened her eyes to ascertain who David was talking to, as was Kim. Looking at the men, Sarah knew she didn't have to be there, she carried Kim off David's body, "I have to take her back before heading home, I'll see you again some other time." David smiled, nodded his head as she walked away.

Looking back at Jack, David asked, "What is this ISIS SHIT about? What did he mean by the world will soon find out who they are? You are asking me questions, but I also have lots of questions of which I think you have the answers, but you are not answering mine."

Jack answered him, "I can't say any more, whatever information I have on this issue is classified and can't be handed down to just anyone."

"Anyone you say, I saw these scumbags up close, I heard their sick desire for attention, I kind of think I passed the position of anyone when I risked my life to save everyone in that shopping mall. You must tell me what's going on? Is there a new terrorist group on the horizon trying to make a name for themselves? Do you mean to say to me that lives were lost, and properties destroyed all in the name of trying to make a name?"

Jack turned to his associates and said, "It is as we feared, it's the same group, we have to head back to HQ, and this is bigger than us."

David, curious about what was going on, tried to involve himself in the conversation Jack was having with his colleagues, "What are you talking about agents? What are your fears? Who are these people? You can talk to me, I'm sure I have some level of clearance."

Jack looked at David, "What do you mean? Do you work with the agency?"

It was unprofessional to give out that information, David refused to say, "I am a British citizen, anything that would put me and other citizens in danger warrants my knowledge. I am willing to do what I can for Britain, but I need to know what you are talking about."

The agents smiled as they walked away, Jack looked back at David and said, "That's not how it works David, but I like your energy, your desire to protect Britain is what we need if we are going to create a safe haven for our children. That will be all for now, if any other question arises, I will be back but for now, get well soon comrade."

David Scarlet wanted so badly to know what was going on, who was behind the attack. There was a dark cloud brewing over Britain, and he felt that keeping Britain safe was something he was good at doing. The only way he could do that was if he got better and got back to work. This seemed like something he could handle. As the four special agents walked away, David laid on his back and turned on his side, facing the wall. He wasn't satisfied knowing that there could be more to the terrorist attack than just the attack on Larimer Square.

He picked up the phone by his side, he had a special number that he was given by the Prime Minister to allow them to talk on sensitive matters. The phone rang and was answered immediately, the Prime Minister spoke, "David, how are you doing?"

"I am in pains, but I am fine sir." David continued, "Sir, I'm not sure but I feel like there's something bigger about this terrorist attack at Larimer, this was just a shopping mall part in a grand scheme. It might be a gut feeling, it might be true, I'm not certain but I really think it should be looked into."

The Prime Minister paid rapt attention to David, "I think so too, and we are already on it, it's an operation I wanted you to take charge of but get well soon and return to

HQ, we are going to do the right thing. I will leave you in charge of this. Dark days are coming in Britain, and we need agents like you with loyalty to the Queen and to your country to illuminate these dark days for us. There isn't much we know about them now, but we hope to find out as time goes on. Britain needs you yet again David. I need you. Save us all once again like you did before and I know you can."

A sensation ran down David's body, duty calls and this time he couldn't get up and respond. The foremost thought in his mind to accept, to fight for Britain like he was fighting for his life. To stop any group that wanted to challenge the sovereignty of his beloved Britain, he told the Prime Minister, Mr. Tyler Blaire, "My loyalty to Britain is unflinching, once I leave this hospital, I will take up this mission and do all that is within my power to restore relative peace to London, all her provinces and the entirety of

Britain. Thank you for the trust you have in me."

The call continued for a while as they talked about other matters, he was still talking when he heard footsteps in the hallway that led to his room. He looked by his side and saw Mark, Laura and Carla walk sluggishly to his room. Mark had Carla on one side and Laura on the other. David tried to go down to support them but he was in too much pain, he grunted and Mark screamed at him from where he was, "Stay still Lad, you trying to rip open the stitches or what? We'll get there when we get there." David didn't like being helpless at all, he always wanted to prove to his family that he had what it took to look after all of them. Seeing his wife in pain didn't sit well with David but he had no power to stop it.

Carla had been falling ill, one sickness at a time, since she got pregnant and needed professional help, something about not putting the life of the unborn child at risk.

David hadn't seen a pregnant woman spend all their pregnancy in a hospital, but he didn't question the doctor as Carla was really advanced before she conceived. David, excited to see his wife, struggled to sit up, Carla had the same eagerness to see him as well.

Carla sat down on the chair beside David, the pair said nothing for the first five minutes before tears started rolling down Carla's cheeks. David used his hand to wipe them off, "Why are you crying?"

She responded, trying to find her words, "Because for the second time in our lives, you were going to walk away from me and our child, at least the first time you planned on returning and you did, although late, but this time, you were not going to. Look at you, all bruised and bashed. I don't like this David, I don't, I need to know that you will be there for me, I need to know that forever I can count on you to stay by my side. If I have this baby, I need to know that while they are young, you'll be there to play your role as the father. Every girl or boy needs her father."

David, not happy for the pains he had caused Carla, held on to her fists, he clenched on tightly like he was holding on for dear life as he said, "I am sorry honey that I have done things that are selfish. I had embarked on ventures with little considerations to how it makes you feel and I'm sorry for that and I promise I'll reduce it but, in this case, I had to do something for the people in the shopping mall else they'd all have died for nothing."

Carla continued talking, "I appreciate a lot that you put the lives of others first, but think about me, about your baby, about my parents, if anything were to happen to you, how do you think we would fare, we love you and hope you can make better decisions next time."

David, calm to Carla's words, had a demand he didn't know how she'd receive. He wanted a baby that he wasn't sure she wanted, he didn't want to upset his pregnant wife. He clenched onto her fist like a suckling child to its mother's breast, "Carla, Mark, Laura, I have a request I need to ask of you, it might not be what you want to hear but it's what I feel I should say here and now."

Carla and her parents listened keenly. Mark was the first to respond, "What is it son? You know you can tell us anything, we'll listen to you and decide as necessary, we love and are here to do what is right for you and Carla."

David sat upright, cleared his throat as he began to speak, "There was a child I met at the Larimer shopping mall, she saw her mom get murdered before her, her father nowhere to be found despite attempts by the metropolitan police to find him." He smiled as he remembered Kim's efforts to save his life, he grunted as a sharp pain shot up his injury, he continued, "She might not have done much but she gave her efforts to save my life when I thought it was sudden death for me, she's out there without a care in the world, without love from anywhere. She has taken a liking to me and wants me out of here so we can spend time together. I'm not imposing on you all, but I just wanted to ask if I could bring her home with us. She's not ours but that wouldn't be a problem, we'll make her feel loved and in no distant time, she will be ours."

Carla, not sure how she felt about the plan, saw David's interest of the child. She smiled gently as she held on to her husband, "I know the desire to have yours has been bothering you but ours is on the way. I know your heart is in a good place and I won't stop you, you can have her over. I promise to take care of her like she is mine." She rubbed her stomach as she smiled sweetly, her beauty piercing through the very essence of David's person. He understood why he fell in love with her and had been in love with her his entire life, she had his best interests at heart and knew what to do to make him happy. It wasn't just her, Mark and Laura knew how to stay on David's good side. The love that radiated across Carla's family was contagious, they weren't his direct family but ever since the demise of his parents, Mark had slid into his life and fitted perfectly. Laura had provided motherly support and had made him not feel the death of his a great deal.

He leaned forward as he planted a gentle kiss down her lips, he raised his head up to see the countenance of Mark and Laura, he was married to Carla, but their feelings meant a great deal to him. Laura said, "You will make a great dad, your love for children is admirable. I hope this child gives you the peace you desire but having a child means extra responsibilities, going away without reason is no longer an option. Every child needs their father, and you need to be there for your child as much as you can."

David wasn't sure the nature of his next mission, he had been out missing his supposed meeting with the Prime Minister and the Director of the GCHQ. He didn't know how available he'd be over the next couple of months, it would be inconsiderate for him to push for the adoption of Kim and leave her upbringing in Carla's hands or that of Carla's parents. He wasn't sure what the next few weeks of his life held. He wasn't sure if they needed him, but he kept an open mind. Serving his country was still paramount but his loyalty to his family was also especially important to him.

CHAPTER SEVEN: KIM

David spent a few weeks at the hospital before he was discharged, his injuries almost healed but he still had to spend more time to rest and heal completely. He left the hospital in a wheelchair, Mark and Laura came by to pick him up. He had refused the wheelchair on the count that he could walk, not as efficient as nor normally, but he did not need any help. The doctor refused. It was hospital policy that patients with his level of damage needed support before allowed to operate as once they were.

David was healing quick physically, but mentally, he was still caught in the incident that happened at the shopping mall. He would occasionally fall prey to the advances of his thoughts, trying to decipher what the terrorist had said and also trying to sort the special agents' statements. He wasn't one to lie on his bum and allow a case as this slide past. When David got home the first day, he dug through the internet trying to find out if any similar attacks had taken place across

Britain with the phrase *ISIS Forever* as the focus.

His enquiry proved useful; trends picked up several attacks scattered across Europe that had one thing similar with all of them. The attackers rumoured to have echoed the mantra *ISIS Forever* just before they took their own lives or escaped from the scene of their attacks. David was on to something, but random terrorist attacks wasn't enough to create a case and he also didn't have authorization to open one. His interest had been aroused. He couldn't rest easy if there was the slightest of chance that this ISIS group could be on the verge of causing problems for Britain.

David sat on his laptop trying to make a case against ISIS when he heard the door open. It was Laura and Mark, but why were they around so early in the day, they had refused to allow him to stay with Carla on the ground that he should rest and get better. He was going to snarl at them when he turned and saw Carla, Laura and Mark standing, locked into each other with not even an inch of space between them.

He wondered what they were up to, no one wanting to spill. They each had smiles on their face so he knew it wasn't something serious. He reached for his crutches as he got up from the chair, limped towards them gently avoiding obstacles, and looked at Carla, who didn't look fit enough to be standing but wanted to be part of the prank. "What is going on with you guys? What are you hiding and most importantly Carla, what are you doing standing up? You look so pale; you should be resting or something not trying to pull a prank on me smiling like you had won the lottery or something."

Carla smiled but she was too weak, and she almost fell on the floor. Mark rushed to her aid, preventing her from falling, exposing what the trip had been hiding the whole time. It was Kim, they had managed to bring her home for him to play with. Excited as he saw the child, he dropped his crutches as he rushed to Carla's aid. He held her dearly as Kim rushed to Carla's side. The child, who was with the family for the first time, held Carla's blouse tightly as she saw Carla struggle to regain herself. Mark and Laura helped Carla to the couch, with little energy, Carla placed her left hand on David's cheeks, "I know how happy the child makes you feel so I decided to push for her adoption myself. She's here now, love her as much as you can and protect her. I was a girl once and I understand the importance of a father in a girl's life and since she has identified you as the one, she wants to be her father, I have no choice than to be her mother. Her papers aren't complete yet, but social services allowed her to stay the weekend on accounts of your heroics, her fondness of you and my application. I know I haven't given you yours, I'm not sure if that's the reason why you want her so much or you just have love for her, but I want you to know that I'll love you both forever."

David looked at his wife who had a tear in her eye, he leaned in and kissed her. "It's not about having mine, it's about the heart on this child, she's only a baby but she knows what it means to look out for someone she cares about. She's not going to replace the child you are having, they are going to grow up together and trust me, I'll have enough love to give to both of them equally." Kim held David and Carla together, she hugged them tight, not wanting to let go for fear that, like her birth parents, they'd go away if she let go.

David looked at Kim, his hands on both sides of her face, her bright blue eyes placed right to show him true beauty inside her eyes. Her hair reached her upper back, she was about seven years old, all she wanted was to be loved. She had seen her mother gunned down; her father not willing to make an appearance. For a child, she had seen more than she should. If David and Carla didn't give her the love she needed, she might end up scarred for the horrors she beheld at her tender age.

Kim looked at David wanting that moment to continue forever, she was an intelligent child who knew more than children her age, she looked at Carla and said, "Can I stay with you and David please, Kim continued her plea, I'll be a good girl I want to stay. David promised I could."

David amused her with some magic tricks he had learned whilst as a young magician, he also played some music on a clarinet. to her.

Carla didn't want to give her false hope, she responded, "I want you to stay with too, I am going to have a baby and you'll have a baby brother. You are going to take care of him and protect him and play with him and you will be happy here with David and myself and Grandma Laura and Grandpa Mark." "It is going to be fun. "she said.

She looked at David, so excited that tears rolled down her cheeks, it was abnormal as David thought it was impossible for children to express such emotions. He wiped it as he spoke to her ever so gently, "I promise I will always be there for you, we are going to have so much fun, he continued "we are going to build playhouses and have tea parties and all sorts of things to do."

He saw her eyes lit up, she was ready for the prospect of being his first child, and she asked eagerly, "Do I have to go back to where I have been staying recently or can I spend the night with you. I want to stay with you." She said.

David nodded as he replied, "You are going to spend the night with us," tomorrow you might have to go back but I promise you, I will come back and bring you home personally."

CHAPTER EIGHT:
MISSION BECKONS

The next few months flew by so fast; David had healed completely and was getting used to life with Kim and Carla, with the latter heavily pregnant. His mind had moved on from the proposed mission he was supposed to embark on for Britain. He had found peace with himself. He didn't know what awaited him as he tried to live his normal life.

David had resumed his work at the GCHQ doing paperwork, not engaging in missions, but something big stood in his front. A mission so big yet so shopping mall that not even top brass of British intelligence needed to know what was going on. He was home alone one Saturday as Carla and Kim had spent the night at her parents. David sat at the porch when car tires screeched in his driveway. Doors opened and closed. He tried to find out who they were without putting himself out there. He had learned to be weary of cars parked in quiet places. He watched from the top floor in his house as five men came down from the cars. They were dressed in black suits and walked towards his door. David wondered who they were.

They headed straight for his front door, he couldn't hide as that would permit them to break or force their way into his house. He wasn't willing to do anything that'd put Carla and Kim in danger. Thoughts filled his heart as he wondered who they were and why they were on his property. They could be members of ISIS sent to abduct him for foiling they attack or for his research into their operations, or they could also be British intelligence officers. From where he was in his house, he could see them clearly and saw that they had with them custom made handguns, he had seen those weapons, but he wasn't sure where.

The guns hidden under their suits, tucked in their trousers gave David a cause for concern, they could be here to kill him for all he knew, and he had so much to live for. Their movements, their communications, their body languages gave the impression that whatever their job was in his residence, they were skilled and were not people to not do their job. He was ready however to take his chance.

He heard the bell ring as he went down quietly to attend to the strange men, he opened the door halfway, careful to not be too exposed to the men whom he didn't know, the first man pulled down his shades and spoke to David, "Is this the residence of one David Scarlet?"

"Who's asking?"

The man with a gentle smile on his face responded, "Britain. We are from MI6 on command to bring you to HQ, there's something that the director thinks you have to hear and be part of."

David's fear had gone away, he felt in his chest that he would be deployed to serve sometime soon, and he wasn't going to give up on the opportunity to do that. He followed the men with no hesitation, boarded the black Escalade, black tint all around the vehicle. David and the agents had mutual respect for each other. He never questioned the authenticity of their claims to working for MI6 before he boarded the vehicle. He never expected MI6 to have plans for him due to his unavailability.

David never believed he should refuse any call to a mission as long as he lived. His sole purpose in life was to defend the integrity of Britain from external as well as internal disturbances. He was always there to stand up for Britain, risking his life as much as he could to ensure that Britain survives whatever situation. However, his escapades in uncovering plots within British intelligence to jeopardize Britain's integrity had left him weary of whom to trust and whom not to.

He entered the car with no hesitation, he had the chance to escape even before the agents approached his door as he had seen them a while before they saw him, but he didn't. He had a gut feeling that following them would do him and Britain a world of good. He sat between two of them at the back of the car, with one up front and the other driving as they headed for MI6 HQ.

The agent that led them sat beside him, his hands always in his side as if he was caressing his side arm. David couldn't tell why he was being overly careful, but David knew that in their line of work, mental and physical alertness was paramount if they were going to make it home at the end of a day's work. He sat at the back seat of the Escalade, in between two of them, he could feel their bodies, trimmed and fitted underneath the suits. The drive was swift, no unnecessary words were said.

A few minutes later, they arrived at MI6 covert office, a shopping mall building that stood in Cloth Fair London, the building looked like it had been there for centuries, but its fine architecture made it stand out among the rest. The car drove into the driveway where David met two extra men standing like they had been expecting them, one of them, opened the door of the vehicle as David came down, the men treated him with so much care, no one mishandling him during the process. He felt like a crown jewel as they made sure he got all that he asked for.

He walked into the old building, his hands in his pocket, this time he was tasked with going in alone, the men stood behind the door as he entered. He walked in, looking at the magnificent designs of the building, the beauty of the exterior of the building could only be challenged by the intricacies of the interior, each detail not standing excessive, for every edge he saw, and he appreciated the finer things. The house was quiet, with the sounds of his feet against the floor producing the only sound that David could hear.

As he walked straight into the building, he heard a door open straight down the hallway, he followed it carefully not allowing himself to be distracted by anything that he saw on the way. David entered the open door and saw two men sitting down, facing each other at a desk, the trim was quiet, and he couldn't tell who they were. He was apprehensive, he didn't know what to expect or what was going on, but he was sure it wasn't a move to kill him else the men that brought him would have. The chances of them successfully killing him had reduced when instead of letting four men do the bidding, they sent him to a room that had just two.

He couldn't tell who they were, but he knew looking at them from afar that they were not the youngest, they were older than he was. He walked towards them slowly, not wanting to do or say anything that would prompt in them the desire to kill him. David got closer to them and the lights in the office came on, it was clearer now, his fears went away, it was the Prime Minister sitting still and facing him was the chief medical officer at MI6, Dr Walter Scott. The pair looked to be engulfed in a conversation, with worry written over each of their faces.

David walked closer, unsure why the Prime Minister had to go through all those problems to invite him when he could have called. He got to the desk and asked the obvious question, "What is going on sir?"

With much worry on the Prime Minister's face, he said quietly, "David, there is a major problem. Sorry we went through the trouble of bringing you here in a fashion that isn't normal to you, but this building is one of our most secret assets. It might stand proudly at Cloth Fair but not too many people in London knows what goes on, we needed to keep you out of prying eyes. We didn't want anyone being into you that's why we went through the lengthy process, I apologize but once you find out why you are here, the way you came would be the least of your concerns."

Curious, David asked, "What do you mean by problem sir? Is it the same problem that madness you request my assistance before the incident at Larimer Square?"

The Prime Minister continued, "Yes, it is, just that it had gotten even worse than it was then."

David was confused, "What is this problem you speak of and how can I be of help?"

The Prime Minister adjusted his chair, sat upright, cleared his throat as he spoke, "The terrorist attack you foiled at Larimer Square was no fluke, it was part of a grand scheme that is recently startling to brew around Europe."

David nodded his head, "I had that suspicion, the leader of the group said something about the world finding out who they were eventually, he even shouted the phrase *ISIS Forever* before he blew himself up. I didn't know what he was talking about, but I did some digging myself and adding the information I collected with what you are saying now makes complete sense. They are a terrorist group that is starting operations in Europe."

The Prime Minister nodded his head as he spoke, "That is the general perspective of the problem but there is more to it that affects Britain directly and it's one we have to stop, it's one that is going to cause great damage to Britain if nothing is done. They have been launching shopping mall scale attacks at different countries in Europe, but we can't help but believe that there is a grand plan. One that would rock the very foundations of this country, the continent and possibly the world." David adjusted his chair as he leaned forward to listen clearly to what the Prime Minister was saying.

The Prime Minister paused to clear his throat and continue speaking, "The attack on Larimer Square some weeks ago at first we thought was the main dish, we sent operatives from all possible military divisions to Larimer to avert the attack, we lost men, civilians and an edifice like the Larimer Square shopping mall, it was a sad day for all of Britain but the true sadness wasn't what happened that day at Larimer but what would happen in the near future as a result of our carelessness on the day of the Larimer Square attack." He brought out a white handkerchief as he cleaned his face. He hadn't said what he was going to, but David could feel from the tensions around the room that it was going to be huge, a problem that could endanger thousands or millions of English lives

.

CHAPTER NINE:
DECLON FIVE

The Prime Minister continued talking, "Like I was saying, the attack on Larimer Square as sad as it was, wasn't the main attack on the day, it was a diversion. With all security personnel in London trying to avert the damages at Larimer Square that happened none the less, a research facility belonging to the MI6 was attacked and nothing else stolen but a powerful chemical, a nerve agent that we call Declon 5. I'm not a scientist but I know that the chemical is terribly potent and in the wrong hands might spell the end for not just Britain but for humanity. I don't know the minute details of the chemical, that's why my very good friend Dr Walter

Scott is here, he'll tell you all there is to tell you about this agent, and I'll brief you on your mission afterward.

Dr Scott moved his chair closer to the table where David could hear him with little difficulty, he picked a glass of water and gulped it down, David knew from the gesture that a lot was going to be said but he was ready. This was his job, saving lives and if it meant sitting down for two whole weeks for briefing, he didn't mind. Scott started speaking, "Declon 5 is a great but terrible asset to the English government. With it, we can end enemies as quickly as possible, but it has the same potency when used against us and now that the enemy has it, we have to be really careful. Declon 5 is a human-made chemical warfare agent classified as a nerve agent. Nerve agents are the most toxic and rapidly acting of the known chemical warfare agents. They are like certain kinds of insecticides called organophosphates in terms of how they work and what kind of harmful effects they cause. However, nerve agents are much more potent than organophosphate pesticides. I know I might have said things that look a little difficult but what I'm trying to say is that this chemical is dangerous when exposed to humans, it has been said to be able to infect the lungs if inhaled and in seconds, the lungs collapse, and it infects the blood as they move through causing total organ collapse in minutes and killing the person that is infected. It is dreadful David and has to be stopped."

David needed all information he could get about the drug, he asked, "Why did we start making this or from where did we get the idea that we needed something this deadly?"

The doctor rested his back on the chair as he braced himself for a little history lesson, he continued, "Declon 5 was invented in Germany in 1938 as a pesticide but when the Second World War came into the picture, it was weaponized by the Nazis to aid their inhumane way of warfare. After their gruesome defeat, operatives of the British military stumbled upon the extremely dangerous chemical and brought it back home for further testing. I know it's not something that we should have at this point in time, but we do and instead of spending time discussing why we have it, we should be discussing how to retrieve it before it causes any damage as its damages would be too difficult to contain.

"Declon is most dangerous because like water it has no taste and no colour, it has no smell David, it has no smell and although it is naturally in liquid form, it can be evaporated and turned into gas. It could be anywhere as we speak in Britain and we wouldn't be able to identify its presence, it could be right here with us in my water that I just drank, and I wouldn't know. It's a killer even more silent than the greatest assassin. It can take lives in their millions, and we'd know nothing about it."

Worried, David asked the million-dollar question, "How do we stop something we can't see or taste? How do we stop something we don't even know where to find?"

The Prime Minister cut in immediately, "It might not be as easy as I will say it now but since we can't find the Declon, we have to find the people that took it, once we have them in our custody, we can pry the information out of them. I don't care by what means, inhumane or not but we have to extract that information from them even if it means picking it from their cold dead bodies, I couldn't care any less." David looked at the Prime Minister who was obviously angry, he could see the anger build from his feet and was already at his head, David smiled half-heartedly. His life had been easy going the past few weeks, but he had been reminded the path that he chose to follow. He smiled as he thought in his heart, *It is better to be aware of the danger and take steps personally to avoid it than to be ignorant and just play into the hands of the terrorists.*

The doctor continued talking, "We got the sample of Declon in 1938 from Germany but apparently the scientist who constructed it might have leaked a sample out before we confiscated the entire thing. We are not sure anybody else saw his notes and all because we have it, but the drug was used some decades after we took it from the lab. In 1994, a village in Japan, Ikagamakure witnessed a significant amount of deaths, the cause very difficult to diagnose as all they could see was an attack of the lungs which moved almost immediately to the entire nervous system and total organ failure in minutes. Test after tests proved that it was Declon as it had the same effects as it had when it was used in '38. A little over a thousand lives were lost in just over a day.

The power of the Declon was seen first-hand. As if that was not enough, a year after, it was used in the neighbouring village of Kagazaki, similar symptoms killing over three thousand people."

Emotions flared in the room, David felt the pressure that oozed from the bodies of both men as they sat together. Tensions had gripped all three of them as they tried to cool off to have a productive meeting. They weren't the enemies so displaying anger within themselves wouldn't do. They needed cool heads to aid their deliberations. The doctor continued, "Tracing Declon is hard, you can never know who's infected until they become really sick and when they get really sick, it becomes almost impossible to bring them back. Injection of Declon is almost certain death."

David didn't like that one bit, and he responded, "So we have a chemical that could kill us all in the hands of someone that has identified as our enemy? Well, the odds aren't on our side. We have to be as quick as possible to stop this."

Dr Scott wasn't done talking, he gulped down water as he continued, "There is a little positive to the story however." He smiled as he said that part.

David was eager to hear that they weren't completely screwed even before they started fighting, "We'll get on with it mate."

The three men laughed as the doctor continued, "Nerve agents, sometimes also called nerve gases, are a class of organic chemicals that disrupt the mechanisms by which nerves transfer messages to organs. The disruption is caused by the blocking of acetyl cholinesterase (Ache), an enzyme that catalyses the breakdown of acetylcholine, a neurotransmitter. Nerve agents are acetyl cholinesterase inhibitors used as poison. That's a tough message for you to understand but all I'm saying is it won't kill a person until just the right amount is ingested or inhaled. A little quantity won't kill unless adequate amount of it is introduced into the body but if they can mass produce then the threat becomes real, it puts us on the brinks of collapse. All these are really frightening but the true fright should come from the fact that those who don't have in them a large amount of Declon to kill them wouldn't even know they are infected with a dangerous chemical, they'd display some symptoms like runny nose, watery eyes, shopping mall pinpoint pupils, eye pain, blurred vision, drooling and excessive sweating, cough, chest tightness, rapid breathing, diarrhoea, nausea, vomiting, abdominal pain, increased urination, confusion, drowsiness, weakness, headache, slow or fast heart rate, low or high blood pressure amongst other things but not death."

David had his head in his hand, despair was setting in, "That's a lot for someone who was just mildly exposed or ingested a little, I can't imagine how those who took in a lot would feel."

The doctor laughed gently as he continued talking, "Heavy ingestion or inhalation is fatal and I wish I could tell you the death would be peaceful, but it won't, it will hurt as hell, but it will be swift. Once someone has ingested or inhaled more than enough, he starts to witness loss of consciousness, convulsions, paralysis, full organ failure leading to death. It's not a friendly drug David, it might be the biggest attack in world history if this is not stopped. The little boy attacks of World War II would have nothing on this particular one. Something has to be done and that is why you have been summoned. This is all we have on the Declon about this time, but I believe it is more than enough from a medical perspective but from an agent perspective, I know I have given you nothing, I apologize for that, but I believe the Prime Minister might have more to brief you on that as I take my leave. I beg you in the name of all you hold dear David, save us, please." He got up, the Prime Minister stretched out his hand for a hand shake as Dr Walter Scott left the office.

The Prime Minister looked at David, silence took over the entire room, he mustered courage enough to speak, "David, I need your help as an agent but first I need your advice as a friend. There was a time it was my life they wanted, if I was asked to trade my life and prevent this current problem, I guarantee you I would have without thinking about it. I am the prime minster, but my life is not worth any bit more than any Englishman or woman out there. I am confused, I had considered contacting the terrorists in a bid to avert this danger that rests about our doors, I wanted to listen to their demands and get this over with. What do you think?"

David didn't like that suggestion one bit, "With all due respect in the world sir, are you mad? Negotiating with terrorists? When did we stoop so low? Doing that would mean the service of every agent that had died in the line of work in their service to the queen and to Britain would be a waste and that would just be terrible. It would bring Britain to her knees and would reduce us to nothing. We would be at the mercy of every terrorist group out there and that is not the image we want for our beloved country. I would give my lifetimes over to ensure that the integrity of this great nation is preserved. I accept this mission even though no mission has been placed before me, I will find this group that threatens Britain, and I will retrieve the Declon 5, and I will make them pay for all their crimes towards Britain."

The Prime Minister, unsure how to respond to David's response, smiled and continued, "I'm sorry you had to see me that way David, I had a lot on my mind and I was letting my emotions get the better of me. Back to business then, the mission is simple,

I'll need you to put together a team of your choosing and attend to the Declon 5 case. You have authority to do whatever you want. The British intelligence will provide you with whatever you want. Please David, Britain needs you, I need you. Do this for us all."

CHAPTER TEN: SARAH CROFT

David left the office, headed back for the entrance of the building where the Escalade and the men that brought him took him back home. He got to his house and decided to head to Carla's parents to see his beloved wife and his daughter Kim. He was about to take a shower and change his clothes when he saw Sarah on the front porch. He rushed over to the door to attend to her.

She had a broad smile on her face as she saw him head for the door, he ushered her in as both sat down to bottles of beers on the kitchen table. She had kept a perfect figure despite not being in active service with Britain's Special Forces. She had her wits about her not afraid of anything, he had his eyes fixed at her the whole time. She smiled gently as she asked him, "What's wrong,

never seen a Special Forces lady before mate?"

He smiled as he responded, "I have, I was simply curious what took you into the service, I can't say it was the money, I don't know maybe the thrill or was it the traveling? Tell me your story Sarah. I'm sure it's going to be an exciting tale."

Sarah smiled as she answered, "I have a complex story, it has its ups and downs but mostly downs. I did see a lot while in active service at the SAS, but I have to say since I have been off, the desire to venture has been in and about me but there was no taste of action. The Larimer Square stack may have claimed lives, but it was the first bit of action I've tasted in years." David looked at her not understanding how someone would crave actions that would put their lives at risk, he wished it'd be always peaceful so he could be with his family but here she was, yearning actions.

He pressed her for the story and eventually she obliged, she began telling the details of her sad past that made him realize why she joined the Special Forces. She had nothing more to chase, so it seemed at the time, and she opted for the force instead of a life of crime. She struggled to say it as she had seen a lot of loss in her life. David listened as she told her story.

"I wasn't born with much, I lost my mom at birth, it was just me and my dad. He barely had my time always focused on his work. I pulled a lot of schemes to get his attention but none amazingly effective. He was running research in the far reaches of Africa, looking for things he didn't misplace. I didn't see the interest he had in that life. I liked the things boys found interest in, I had no interest in ancient tombs and treasures, I preferred guns and explosives and their likes but that clearly constructed a ridge between me and my father. Our difference in preferences didn't allow us to agree completely. My dad died in some freak accident somewhere in the jungles of Congo when I was ten and for some reason, I didn't feel sad. His loss wasn't a loss to me, it was no different than I already lived. I had never had a father in my opinion."

David had developed an interest in her story, he adjusted his seat as he gulped down from his bottle of beer. She continued speaking, "I lived with my grandmother until I was twenty or so, I joined the British Army and was posted to Special Forces. I had my training camp in Wales, it wasn't easy a single bit, but it was worth every single bit of it, if I didn't have an immediate family to die for, I might as well put my life on the line for Britain, it was a course I was happy to do over and over again. The training was intense, but I handled it somehow, I made friends that I was willing to die for, it was a rollercoaster training for the Special Services."

David liked her devotion to protecting Britain, he had always thought it was something that he loved to do alone but living in Britain, he had seen a large number of youths who loved the country enough to lay down their lives for it, "I don't reckon you still keep tabs with those friends you made in Wales?" her expression seemed a little as he asked the question.

The smile that she had while telling the story went its way, "I served two tours in Afghanistan with the same team, team nerd troopers, that's what we were called. We weren't just soldiers, we weren't just friends, we were family, the first two happened smoothly, nothing to report, maintained the peace, did what we had to, all six of us went in and came out clean. I thought in my heart that that was how all future operations would be, the Special Forces were a dream for me, I had found a purpose, it wasn't what my father and grandmother, and late mother would have wanted for me, but it was what I wanted for myself. I was living in harmony with strangers, the unity I demanded from my family but couldn't get, I was getting from my brothers."

She sighed and drank her beer as she tried to opt out of telling the story, David leaned in suggesting he was listening and she shouldn't stop, he said to her, "We all have our stories, and it might not be what we want it to be but it's ours and nobody else's. We have to be proud of who we are and how we lived our lives."

She found renewed strength in his sayings as she continued speaking, "My second tour at Afghanistan didn't have the same outcome as the first, the brothers and myself went out to maintain the peace as we did usually but halfway there, new orders came. We were to partner another squadron to an opium plant that was believed to be owned and ran by the Al-Qaeda, it was a major hit as we had been on a losing streak against the terrorists for weeks, higher-ups didn't take a serious look at the cons of the operation, it was just a means of revenge for them. We plunged the depths of the opium plant and true to intel, there were hostile stationed all over the place and it was the worst mission I had been in my entire life."

David tried to cut in to give her the space she needed to catch her breath and not break into tears from having to tell how her comrades fell before her very eyes but she wouldn't have him, she was already telling the story and the best he could do was let her finish, she continued, "There was persistent gunfire, we had the element of surprise but they had the numbers and ammunition, we held our end, pushing them back and gunning a large chunk of them but the loss on our end was massive. We were twenty-two that went out on the mission, we recorded fifteen deaths of which my brothers in arms were aiming, four injured, and just three unscathed. I was unharmed but I had lost my team, not that the rest of the military wasn't my team but the six of them formed a major part of not just my military presence but my life generally. I got back to base unhurt, but I wasn't myself anymore."

She stopped talking for a while, David had brought before her a bottle of water which she picked up, gulped down a significant portion, and continued talking, "I was given time off after the loss of my team to recuperate, brought back home to London to undergo some military psychological restructuring or something to lit me back to tip-top shape. I spent two years back in London before I was shipped back to the Middle East, this time it wasn't to Afghanistan but this time to Iraq in an operation called operation Teliq, I arrived in Iraq on 12 March 2003, where I joined up with a different squad, the Special Forces were to aid in the invasion of Iraq. It was a barrage of missions, I joined up with the D-squadron, and our job was to support the coalition advance on Basra, to conduct forward route reconnaissance and to infiltrate the city. We got information that the Ba'athist loyalist would be meeting up with their leaders at Basra and we had to stop them from plotting further. It was a clean sweep as we lost no soldier in the process. It was warfare like I had imagined yet again. There was no rest for us, after that we were deployed to secure the intersection of the two main highways linking Baghdad with Syria and Jordan."

David cut in, "It seems you had quite an eventful service to your country. You healed quickly from the demise of your friends, but didn't you lose any other after they died?"

Sarah smiled as she moved to answer his question, "I learnt a lot, but for all the valuable lessons, death was inevitable, soldiers were going to die and it was part of our job description, I had to move on and keep fighting. I understood that they were giving their lives for the greater good. Don't interrupt me again Mr Man. The biggest test of my special force career was when we had to support agents of MI6 into Baghdad for their mission which was branded top secret. It wasn't so secret, I guess there was a mole in the British military, but it didn't end well on the day. We encountered massive resistance, claiming more military lives than I had ever seen in my life. It was at that point that I decided to draw the curtain on my Special Forces career. I served that tour somehow and came back to London. It had been rather quiet in London, but it was worth more than seeing friends die on a daily basis."

She had lost a lot in service of her country but in her, David saw a woman who would willingly lay down her life for her country, she had ticked all his boxes and he knew in his heart that bringing her on board his current mission wasn't an action he'd regret. She had the skill set and from what he saw at Larimer, she had the tenacity to survive tricky situations and the willingness to fight and bleed for her country. He had no other option, he said to her, "Sarah, I have heard and seen you for who you are but you barely know me." Her head was down but when he said that, she raised it up staring straight into his eyes as she began to wonder what sort of man he was. What regular man would sustain so many injuries to save the lives of people he barely knew, she now wanted a story, an explanation of the background he had.

David saw in her eyes the desire for explanations but said as calmly as he could, "I could start to tell you a lengthy story about my life but I won't, I'm going to pick out the part that are important and let you know before I table arguably the most important issue in all of Britain right now before you." She paused not understanding all that he was saying. He cleared his throat as he continued, "I know you have your suspicions and it is exactly right that you do, my name is David Scarlet, and I work as a senior security man, but my story transcends beyond. I have seen you risk your life for people hence the need to say to you what I am saying now. I am an agent with the GCHQ—"

"I knew it, no ordinary man would go through the lengths you went through and as professionally done as you did it, there had to be something about you but a spy? I wouldn't have guessed."

He smiled as he continued, "I served at Saudi Arabia many years ago and in Russia a few years ago. I have been deactivated for a while, but I was recently reactivated. Before I say anything, how do you feel about saving Britain and maybe the world?"

She laughed as she responded, "What do I look like to you, the *Avengers* or what? I couldn't even save my fallen comrades, how can I save the world?"

David laughed, "I have saved Britain a couple of times so I know a thing or two about it, I am creating a team for a mission so secret that if it slipped from your mouth, I might have to kill you myself." She gasped. "I wouldn't kill you, I was only joking but you never know. The mission is so top secret that nobody else outside of this room and a handful of others knows about its existence. You have mentioned twice how bored you have been since you left the Special Forces. Here is a task for you and I guarantee you that it would give you all the thrill you desire and maybe even more and have no fear, you won't lose comrades this time, I promise."

She drank what was left of her water as she laughed, "You have a bad habit of making promises that you have no control over, you can't say for sure that I won't lose comrades, I might be the one to go this time, but I like how you tried to make me calm. You wanted to attack my fears. I'm in, I don't care the details but seeing you at the shopping mall protect all those lives, I know for sure that I can place mine in your hands and it is guaranteed to be safe. That doesn't mean I don't want to know what we are getting ourselves into you know?"

David sat upright, adjusting himself so he could whisper the details of the mission to her, she could barely hear him but that was how classified the mission was, "I don't know the details, but we will find out but there's a terrorist organization in Britain and they have acquired a chemical weapon so fierce it can end life as we know it in Britain. That's as much as I know but if you agree to join me, we will get details at a briefing that is supposed to happen in two days as long as I have been able to assemble a team of five myself inclusive."

"I am in, I'd love more than anything to protect Britain and I would want to do it under you. You might not think much of it, but you inspired me a great deal at Larimer Square the other day. A secret spy? I pictured you in many ways but not ones as a spy, aren't you a little old to be doing something this dangerous, especially with a baby on the way and your recently adopted baby girl. I am not saying there wasn't enough reason to hand you the mission, but wouldn't you rather just enjoy life with your family?"

David stood up from his seat, "You can only enjoy life if there is a life to be enjoyed. The safety of our home is under threat, and you want me to enjoy life with my family. You might not get the full picture, but I guarantee you that when you get the full briefing, you'd know that if this attack isn't yearned, there will be no life to enjoy. The streets of London will be filled with corpses but none of us will be able to tell how many are dead because we'd all be dead ourselves. If they use the weapon they have, everyone would die, every social strata would be affected, the rich, the poor, teachers, doctors, politicians, artists, you name it, we'd all be done for. I can't enjoy my life when I know a threat that big rests around the corner. I need to stop this then I will enjoy what's left of my life with my family."

Sarah had no response, she kept quiet as she saw the emotions pouring out of every pore In David's body, she looked at him with admiration as he said to her, "With you on board, I know the two others I am going to recruit, it's not going to be easy one bit but if it was, it wouldn't be what we want right? But we are going to get it done, we are going to restore Order and punish these assholes that seek to destroy Britain."

CHAPTER ELEVEN:
FAMILY

Sarah left David's house hours after she arrived. A dark cloud brewed across Britain. The terrorists could strike at any time and put all of Britain in total mayhem. David was going to fight back but for now, he had the next two days to report back to MI6 with a complete team, he had his sights set on the complete members of his team. He had Andrew Charlton on one side, a friend and spy, and the pair joined the service together in the late seventies. Andrew had proved himself useful to the queen uncovering terrorists' agenda in the British military in the nineties, he was among a team of covert spies who uncovered a plot to sabotage Britain by the Germans. He had his day but decided that his spy days were over. He lives with his family at Liverpool, owns a pawn shop and is doing rather fine. David wanted him at all cost for his quick thinking and his ability to make a plan in the tightest of situations.

He also had Roger Moore on his sights, he had always admired the childwho the agency calls the super spy. His records preceded him, his excellence in achieving results matched only by the grace with which he carried himself. He was a true genius of the art. His handling of a weapon could only be rivalled by the spectacle that he was whenever he put on a suit. David had always wondered why he had the same name as one of the characters that played James Bond. He never asked, the question felt awkward but maybe working together would give him the opportunity to ask the super spy.

He had Josh McGee, a spy in the GCHQ, known for his understanding of explosives, it had been rumoured that Josh could sniff a bomb a thousand miles away. David knew that had Josh been at the Larimer Square shopping mall, the explosives wouldn't have gone out. It wasn't a tough decision adding Josh to the team, he had seen what ISIS did with explosives and having a bomb specialist would be useful. Josh wasn't just anti-explosives, he had a nose to sniff out any substance poisonous to man, gas leakages and what not. David wasn't sure but if anyone was going to identify the Declon 5, it would be John. But John was always involved in a mission at all times, it would be difficult to bring him into his team as the man was as scarce as they come. David was determined, knowing he had no other option than to bring him into the team.

He already had Sarah Croft on his team, the only one among them who wasn't a spy but had tactical experience, she had served in various places around the world maintaining peace and could as well contribute to their goal. She wasn't as inventive as Andrew neither was she as glorious as Roger but she had her perks, her tenacity reached for the heavens. She was as physical as Andrew was technical. Being the only woman in the team, she was the muscle. He liked her devotion and that was more than enough reason to recruit her.

He had his team and all he had to do was to convince the others to join him, Roger wouldn't be an issue, all he had to do was explain the gravity of the mission and how solving it would increase his super spy status and like a loyal dog, he'd join with little complaint. He already had Sarah on board, his only problem would be Andrew and Josh, it would be difficult to convince a retired agent to go back into the field and it might be even harder to find Josh in London. Andrew would have gotten used to his life as a family man and might not be open to returning to the hazards of the everyday spy lifestyle. This was going to be his life for the next few weeks or months or so he thought.

He wasn't sure how long it'd take but a move to stop an operation like this that had roots spread around Europe wasn't going to be easy.

He knew his fate and knew that he had to spend some time with his family, he wondered what excuse he could give this time to Carla, Laura, Mark and Kim. He went straight for Mark's the instant Sarah left. He should spend the next two days with his family as he wasn't sure where the mission would carry him to or when he'd be back. He walked in and saw Carla and Kim together, making a dress. The picture was perfect, just like he had imagined life would be. He couldn't hear any other sound in the house creating the impression that Mark and Laura were not around at the time. He walked straight to Carla who saw him and rushed to hug him, Kim followed and hugged his legs as she could barely touch his body, he carried her up in his arms as he planted a gentle kiss on his wife's lips.

He held on to them both as though he feared they could be taken away, Carla wasn't sure why, so she asked him, "What is going on David? Are you going anywhere, is anything the problem? What's with this hug?" He laughed as he said nothing, he just tightened his grip as he smiled.

Kim had been with him for weeks, but she loved them like she was their child by birth, she replied to Carla, "I don't know why he's hugging us this much, but I think it is because he loves us and don't want to let us go."

David finally said words in response to Carla's curiosity, "Can't a man just hug two of the most important ladies in his life without a reason, I missed you and decided to hug my queen and my princess."

Carla with a smile on her face replied, "You missed us? You almost slept here last night, you only left when daddy asked if you weren't going to. I know you David and I think there's something up, that's why you are showering us with all this love, so we close our mouths, if that's it, it won't work." David walked to the couch, sat down with the remote in his hands, Kim still holding him firmly like she wasn't interested in letting go, she brought out books with cut outs that needed to be painted. She finally let him go as she rushed over to get some crayons for her to paint.

Carla sat down close to David, "I know you, what is going on? I fear you want to leave us again?" He remained quiet for a while not wanting to say anything that could ruin the moment, he had a family, he had them together and he wasn't going to lose them again.

"I might go away for some time for work but not like the last time, I am here, I will always be here for the both of you."

Carla was about to get up from the chair and walk away in anger when Kim held her hand as she attempted to stand up, she was just a baby, but she had a sixth sense that Carla didn't have, she said, "Mom, I know you don't want daddy to go but he has to. But he should promise us that he won't take too long because I know he keeps his promises."

David, with a tear in his eye, nodded his head as if to suggest he wouldn't take long. He couldn't allow anything happen to them, he was going to protect them and all of Britain. The three of them sat there quiet, nobody saying anything with Carla shedding tears and Kim just wanting the crying to end. They were like that for a while before David broke the silence, "I want us to have a wonderful day. You both should get dressed, we are going out to London Square for a father, mother and daughter time. This is how a family should be and this is how I intend to make mine. There'll always be smiles on our faces because we will always be together in love and unity."

They left the house for the park, children running around the park, having an enjoyable time with their parents. Kim quickly settled in as she found some children her age to play with. Carla sat down troubled that David was going away yet again, she worried within, *Why does he always go away when I am with child. I want him to be with me and share the experiences, but he never is. He does this for us or so he says, I either have to believe him and stay strong for us or not and go away with my child.* She was not happy with his news.

David was with Kim as she made her way through a shopping mall castle constructed with LEGO, she was having the time of her life. He wished for a second that Carla would be like the child. David got up from Kim's side, he told her in her ears, "Hey baby, daddy will be right back, I have a thing or two to talk to mommy about." The child nodded her head as she kept on playing with the other children. David stood up, heading to where Carla was seating when he saw Roger Moore and his girlfriend trying to have a bit of time together. He could either try to pacify Carla or work towards saving Britain.

It wasn't a tough choice as the latter won with little hassle, he changed trajectory as he walked towards Roger, Carla looked at him from afar as she saw him approach Roger. Roger stood up from his seat to receive the spy legend that approached him. Roger said something to his girlfriend in her ears as she stood up, when David got close, he greeted David as he said, "Good morning sir, what are you doing here?"

David responded, "I'm here with my family, just trying to have a quiet day with them, who's the lovely lady you sit here with?"

Roger quickly continued, "Pardon my manners, this is Sam, Samantha Edgeworth, she is my girlfriend, we just came out together for a wonderful time."

David stretched out his hand to shake hers and she did as well, "Nice to meet you Sam."

She replied, "Likewise."

They shared a few words exchanging smiles before David demanded some personal time with Roger, "Dam, I'm sorry for interrupting but there's something of utmost importance that I have to talk to Roger about and it is really personal. I don't know if I could borrow him for a short while. I promise to bring him back in the same shape as I had taken him." She laughed as she allowed them walk away. David and Roger walked together as they headed away from the benches.

Roger was eager to know why the legend needed him, "What is going on sir?"

David had his hands on Roger's shoulders when he started to speak, "Son, there is trouble, one so big and so fierce that if not put out, will bring Britain to the brink of extinction."

Surprised at his response, Roger wanted to believe he was only joking, "It can't be that bad, can it?"

David didn't smile back when he asked the question. "There is a terrorist organization that is sweeping through Britain and through Europe. I saw their works first-hand at the Larimer Square attack, they were behind it and the Prime Minister seems to think they have a hold on a weapon that could prove costly. I have not the complete details, but I've been tasked with setting up a team that could help stop this menace. If we don't stop it, millions could die in London and hundreds of millions across Europe and maybe even billions around the world. I know it might be sudden, but the mission begins tomorrow, and I have handpicked you to be among my team, you carry yourself with so much grace and your success rate is abnormal for one so young.

Would you do me the honours and join my team, we have to save Britain."

Roger stopped for a second to process his thoughts, "I'm in sir, this looks like the biggest test yet for my glittering career. The intention is to be bigger in real life than James Bond was in the movies. Plus, British lives are in danger, it's not just a job anymore, it's something I have to do to secure English lives. I have no other purpose in life but to protect and serve. I might look like I do it for the glam, but I do for honour, for loyalty."

David liked what he was hearing, he laughed as he asked a question, "What is your story child? I'm just asking to be sure I am setting up the right team."

CHAPTER TWELVE:
ROGER MOORE X
ANDREW CHARLTON

The pair sat down on another bench as Samantha had gathered a handful of children, Kim inclusive and was teaching them a song. David and Roger looked at the scene, this was what they were fighting for, the love, the togetherness that flowed through the English people. The freedom to make live choices, the desire to protect and provide for each other. He looked back at Roger. "What prompted you into the spy life? I can't say it was the fame because there isn't any. Regardless of what you achieve, your name is hidden from the papers and the news reports, movies could be made about you with no one knowing who exactly prompted that movie. It's not the life that fits a youth of your personality trait, so what pushed you into it."

Roger looked at Samantha, "I had options sir, I could be whatever I wanted to be but I chose this life for two reasons. Firstly my dad worked with MI6, I found out my dad was a spy when I was fifteen, he wasn't supposed to let me know he was a spy but it slipped and I found out. Norshopping mally kids would be too excited about their fathers being like James Bond or something and go around blabbing to other children but I found myself keeping the secret. I said nothing to no one and I started dreaming of a future where I was a spy like he was. I had it all as a child, the game, the face, the physique and my father provided me with all I needed to live a happy life, but I found myself tutoring towards the spy dream. I went to school like every other boy, I attended Harvard, bagged a degree in criminal law, I started working with a firm, but I couldn't stay focused for long because I wasn't living by the dream that I wanted."

Intrigued by his story, David asked him, "What was the second reason why you opted to be a spy?"

"You'd expect me to be a bully by virtue of the fact that I had it all as a child and not many children came close to me in terms of success in educational career, but I found myself wanting to help people David. I opposed my teammates lots of times because they wanted to bully people but I never wanted that. I would go to unimaginable ends just to ensure that nobody gets hurt on my watch. I knew what path I had to follow, I spoke to my dad when I was in the university of Liverpool about my desire to join the agency. He was surprised but he knew I wasn't going to take no for an answer so he asked me to complete my studies and he'd see what he could do.

When finally I was through with school, I made my way into the service. I've had a colourful career and my dad would be super proud of me if he were here but that wasn't the reason why I signed up. I didn't do it to get my father's attention, I signed up because I wanted to protect people and serve the queen in my capacity, I'm not going to stop because I've made my father proud, I'm going to stop when I can no longer do it physically. I appreciate your handpicking me amongst a plethora of other dazzling agents, it means I am doing the right thing. I promise not to let you down sir."

He had so much respect for David, he stretched out his hand to shake David's. David still had questions to ask, "Are you on any mission currently?" Roger shook his head to gesture he wasn't as David continued talking, "By the start of the day after tomorrow, we will be going for mission briefing as time doesn't side with us, I have to let you know, every other mission you have succeeded in in your rather fancy career, no one matches to this. It's so classified that even some top brass in the service know nothing about it, you mustn't let anybody know else I'll kill you myself. If information this goes out, panic will sweep through all of Britain, and it'd make the case ten times harder to solve. We need the masses oblivious of what is going on." Roger nodded his head, he knew how it worked, and he wasn't new to the game.

David smiled, "I have to ask child, why are you named after a James Bond character? It has been in my mind since I met you, I am sure you get that a lot but really I have to know."

Roger laughed out loud, "Moore is a family name, I do agree that the addition of Roger to it was a function of the James Bond movies. My father was a huge fan of the franchise and being a spy himself, it made absolute sense calling me Roger Moore. I am sure my father always wanted me to be a spy hence the name and letting me find out what he does for a living and I am grateful he did. I wouldn't trade this line of work for anything in the world."

"In two days', time, we'd need you for briefing, not to worry where, you will get there when the time is right. Go back to your girlfriend child, have all the time you can with her, show her as much love as you can for after now, we venture into uncharted waters trying to rescue a drowning Britain. I am happy you are on board. I respect you just as much as you respect me, you are the present and future of the espionage game, I will keep you safe, I promise." Roger walked back towards where Samantha was as David looked at him from behind. *Even without a suit, he carries himself with some level of pride, he likes what he does and that is what you need from a secret service agent. It should never be about the pay check or the fame, it should be about the passion, the love for one's country and the desire to protect the people that matter most to them, he's third generation spy and all through his family line, they've oozed brilliance, he's a legacy and I know that he had a lot to offer to the secret service. I hope he lives up to the hype and becomes an even greater agent than his father and his grandfather before him.*

As Roger walked away, David knew his team was almost complete, but he had to contact Andrew if he was going to get his team selection complete before the day of briefing. He brought a shopping mall paper from his pocket with Andrew's number written on it, he brought out his phone and dialled the number. It rang for a few seconds, and it was picked up, he spoke carefully not wanting Andrew to figure who was speaking from the get-go. Andrew spoke first, "Hello, who is this?"

"It's an old friend, just calling to see how things are with you."

Andrew wasn't feeling it, "Doesn't this old friend have a name?"

David laughed a little and said, "If you can't figure that out, I'm going to be really offended, you old goat."

It was as if the mention of old goat juggled his memory, Andrew responded immediately, his voice hitting new heights, "David Scarlett, as I live and breathe. I thought you'd be dead by now, what business do you have being alive?"

The pair both laughed simultaneously as the call continued, David answered, "I always told you I'd go after you. You are the reason I'm still around, whenever you finally exit the earth, I will start thinking about doing the same."

Andrew laughed as he spoke back, "What's up, how's the family, the job?"

"It's not been the worst. Taking it one day at a time."

"It's been forever we had a conversation, you missing me already?"

"I wish I was, I need your help Andy, something has come up that I need your help with."

Silence overtook the call as both men waited to see who'd continue speaking, Andrew broke the silence, "You know I've moved on from that life right, I'm trying to see out my days with my family."

"See out your days mate? You are just fifty, and knowing you, I know you have no plans of dying, your children might have to beg you or do it themselves for you to finally leave the earth."

Andrew laughed, "What's going on?"

David cleared his throat as he continued, "I don't know if you heard of the Larimer Square attack?"

"Who didn't? It was all over the news."

"Good, that attack was a distraction, the Prime Minister mentioned that it was a distraction to obtain something from MI6's vault, they took a chemical called Declon 5."

"You keep saying they, who are they? And what does this have to do with me?"

David had to be really convincing if he was going to get Andrew on board, "They are a newly formed organization, they call themselves ISIS, we are not sure who they work for or their goals and aspirations but they were behind the attack at Larimer Square to distract security operatives from their real mission, infiltrating MI6 safety vault, something whose location is classified. It's safe to say they have eyes in the right places and they are using them very well. Declon 5 is a nerve agent that could end life as we know it or send a significant amount of English men and women and children to hospitals for extended periods or maybe kill them in a matter of minutes. They have this nerve agent and there's belief that they haven't used it yet because they might be trying to mass produce. Now how this concerns you, I have been given a task to set up a team to make enquiry and investigation into this matter and solve it finally. I am hoping to talk you into returning back to active duty in service to your country and to the queen and to help me solve this grave problem that plagues is once and for all. After this, I will actively support your retirement plans as I will be retiring myself. Let's foray this one time into espionage and go out with a bang."

The silence returned as David waited patiently for Andrew's reply, "Why would I come back? This problem is for the British government to fix, they should know why a terrorist organization seeks out lives. The groups must have made demands, and if they know then they should do something about the demands and keep us all safe."

"Andrew, this isn't about government and demands, this is about innocent lives, you never know, your loved ones could be the first exposed to the Declon 5, and how would you feel if they die or get really sick? It's about protecting the country we love, I know the fire for Britain burns deep in your heart and I beg you to please not turn your back on your country. Larimer Square showed up what this ISIS can do, they have no mercy, they will attack and it's not just the government that would withstand the worst of the attack, we all will so please come out old friend, join me and help us rid our home of this bastards." The silence still lingered as Andrew said nothing. David continued, "Mission briefing is in two days, you are one of the best agents I've seen out there, I could have picked any young agents to support me but your methods, the numbers stand in your favour, you can help me out, please don't let me down. Thank you, I really do hope you think about it."

He was going to drop the phone when Andrew responded, "This is the last foray for me and for you?" David replied positively before Andrew continued,

"Protecting Britain was the dream, but we have lost too many friends to the dream, I still want to give my life for Britain, but we aren't as young as once we were, it's going to be difficult for us."

"Physicality isn't always it, your ingenuity can be matched by none I have met, you can, we can do this."

Andrew sighed, "Okay, I will join you, let's fine together one last time after which we bow out in style."

"That's the Andrew I know, we will be fine, I will keep the entire team safe, I promise."

"Still promising, are we? I intend to keep you safe this time. Tell me mate, who else makes up the team?"

David laughed, "You are not going to like this one bit, there's this new child who everyone calls the super spy, I picked him for his numbers. He is Shawn Moore's child, he might be a little too much personally but he's a third-generation spy and he's got skills."

Andrew responded in shock, "The great Shawn Moore? The childlearnt from the very best, no wonder you handpicked him for the team, who else?"

"The other member isn't an agent per se, she's SAS, Special Forces, served two tours in Afghanistan and Iraq, she was with me at Larimer and helped me put a stop to the attack."

"You were at Larimer Square the day of the attack?"

"I was there, with Sarah's help, I could demobilize the terrorist and establish communication with the security operatives around, but the terrorists blew themselves up before questions were asked."

"I'm guessing the fourth member is named Sarah, who else is on the team?"

David continued, "It's a four-man team, it's going to be easy to discover. The operations of ISIS spread beyond Britain. We are going to have to locate them to the crannies of Europe, it promises to be fun but going to be really risky. I need you to bring your A-game. I just want to end this once and for all and go back to life with my family."

The call continued as the pair continued to talk about other things, Andrew continued talking, "How's Carla? Your father, your mother, your spasms?"

David was indifferent, "Carla is with child, and I also adopted a child I saved at Larimer Square. My father and my mother died some time ago, a car accident, but Carla's parents have filled the void making me feel like I never lost anyone. As for my spasms and random speeches, they stopped after series of physiotherapy, neurological tests and drugs upon drugs, I am finally free, I have been my one man, reactivated into the service. It has been a rollercoaster period for me, and I aim to top it off with this which will be my final contribution to the secret service. I am getting too old for this anyway. How's Joanna and Liverpool. I'm not a football fan but I know you must be glad about Steven Gerrard's march to the champions' league final?"

Andrew laughed, "Joanna is fine, and Liverpool is amazing. You've never been a fan of football, it's been two years since the famed miracle of Istanbul, just so you know, we came pretty close yet again this year, but it wasn't to be. The Milanese side had their revenge and funny enough, it didn't hurt as much as I thought it would."

The pair laughed as David said, "I have to go, I've been away from Carla and Kim a while and the goal we had in mind was to come here and bond as a family."

"Kim, who's Kim?"

"The child I adopted. I hope to see you in two days' time mate, be safe." He dropped the call as he used his eyes to search for Carla and Kim. They sat together locked in each other's arms as it looked like Carla was singing to Kim. He stood up from the chair he was sitting, he walked close to them as he held them firmly from behind, his hands locked as he kissed Kim gently on her forehead and Carla on the nape of her neck.

He wished the moment wouldn't go away but he was sure it would, he understood that what he was doing was for the greater good. If only he could tell them and make them understand as well. He wondered that being a spy wasn't a problem, it was merging it with being a family man that was the problem. He cleared his thoughts, "I should enjoy every moment left with them and not live in my own thoughts even as I spend time with the two most important persons in my life." He held them tight not wanting to let go, the things that mattered were around and letting go wasn't an option. If only.

CHAPTER THIRTEEN:
JOSH MCGEE

The hardest one to find of all the members that David had proposed to be on his team, Josh had engagements round the clock as his instinct and knowledge of substances made him a valuable set to British intelligence. David made calls through to the director of operations at the GCHQ trying to get a hold on Josh, but he had been blown off on the premise that he was on a really classified mission. David considered giving up on Josh and replacing him with someone else, but none would fill his role. He was irreplaceable.

He had been trying to get through to Josh. He had left him messages, calls, even been to his house a couple of times hoping to see Josh but all efforts failed as the ever-busy Josh returned none of his calls. David was becoming frustrated but his devotion to the cause had identified Josh as the man he needed, and he was going to keep trying until he was sure that he couldn't get Josh.

He got home from the park with Carla and Kim and went up to the fridge to get a cold bottle of beer when he heard sounds. He heard someone make a move across his back porch, he reached for his 9mm handgun that he had hidden perfectly in a shopping mall compartment behind his kitchen cabinet. He checked the cartridge for rounds as he carefully walked towards Carla and Kim. He hid his gun as he told Carla that he heard sounds and they should head for the basement. He slowly headed for the back door, tipping his toe not wanting to be noticed, he opened the door carefully as it made a creaking sound. He saw no one as the place was pitch black. He moved backwards just enough so his hands could enter his kitchen while his body remained outside, he flipped the light switch and in front of him was Josh McGee, the man he had been looking for.

Josh had an expression on his face to suggest he found David's response to his disturbance funny. "I heard you've been looking for me everywhere mate, what is the problem?"

Sitting on a shopping mall white chair, a man, fit for his forties with short blond hair, blue eyes, broad shoulders and freckles all over his face. David lowered his gun as he responded, "It's pretty hard to find you these days Josh."

Josh laughed as he stood up, "I have been around, I don't think this is the best place to have this conversation, meet me at the Open Clam Bar, a few blocks away. I reckon you know it, right?"

They shook hands and David replied, "I do, I'll be there in ten minutes, just have to put my wife's mind at ease and I'll be with you."

Josh smiled as he took of his hat to salute David and walked away, "Say hi to the missus will you?"

He was an unpredictable character, David thought as he looked at him walk away. He could take nothing serious, but he had a tremendous record in the agency. The British intelligence is saturated with decent ages but none more spontaneous than Josh McGee. David tucked his gun in his trousers as he went back into the house. He headed straight for the basement where Carla and

Kim were hiding. Carla came out when she saw that it was him, "What was that?"

David smiled as he said to her, "It was just my imagination, I am sorry for scaring you." Carla and Kim came out as David walked back upstairs. He walked up to Carla as he told her that he had somewhere to be, she never knew him to be someone who had friends he went out with, but she had no complaints.

David met Josh at the Open Clam just in time. Josh, who always had a smile on his face regardless the situation, asked David in his usual playful manner, "What is the problem? You have been looking for me a while now, I'm here."

David adjusted his seating position as he leaned forward towards Josh, "I know you are a busy man and all but there is something very important that you must do with me. It's a mission and I need you on this one."

"I know it's a mission but what is it about?"

"There is a terrorist organization making her move on Britain and Europe. We are not sure what they want yet but we have an idea what they have already, and it could prove to be really dangerous for us if they make use of what they have."

Josh was already interested, he drank from his bottle of beer that stood on the table the whole time, he said to David, "Pardon my manners, I didn't offer you anything, what can I get you?"

"This is not the time for beer, but for work. Like I was saying, on the day of the Larimer Square shopping mall demolition, something was stolen from MI6's bio-lab, a chemical, a nerve agent Declon 5." Josh didn't sound surprised, it felt to David like he knew the chemical and that was good news, for them to get any close to finding it out, Josh had to know what he was talking about, David cut in, "You know about Declon 5?"

Josh nodded his head, "I do, I was doing a study of all chemical weapons we have at the agency, and I stumbled upon it, it was dastardly as I could make no clear assertion on its door, it had no colour. It was impossible to identify. Hmm, this sounds like it's going to be a sticky pickle."

David shook his head as he said to Josh, "I'll have a drink about now."

Josh smiled as he signalled the waiter to bring a bottle of beer, the kind he was drinking, David continued, "I was tasked with setting up a team to put ISIS down and stop her operations in Britain first. I have assembled my team and I think you'd make a great addition to the team, your skill sets are unique to you and I'd love it if you joined us." Josh nodded his head positively suggesting he'd join them in taking down ISIS.

David looked at him a while and spoke up yet again, "If you don't mind me asking, what's your story? I look at you every day and every day I'm unable to profile you. What about you to find out than from you?"

Josh laughed out loud before he responded, "I try to make myself as unpredictable as I can, I am not one with a beautiful childhood, I grew up practically by myself. My father was a mad man, my mom died when she had me. I struggled trying to create a bond with my father who around the time I was eight was arrested for murder, multiple counts. He was an arsonist, he spent all his time in our basement mixing chemicals and what not to make explosives and thinking of weird ways to start fires. It was the worst way to grow up. I am surprised I didn't give to crime."

He paused for a second, looked at David, "I hope I'm not boring with all my stories, I get a bit theatrical when I do things even when I talk." David laughed and shook his head,

Josh continued his story, "I was eight, got home from school and saw my father packed like he was going on vacation but his luggage wasn't stacked with clothes, it was with explosives and stuff that he needed to blow up an entire city. I asked where he was going to but I never got a response, he left that day and never returned, he was arrested months later. He was the orchestrator of the Birmingham fire that killed forty in eighty-four." He ordered yet another beer as his throat was dry from telling his sad story, he continued, "I basically had to bring myself up, from orphanage to orphanage, I never knew how people found out that I was the child of a monster, I never got adopted. When I was eighteen, I left foster care and had to make it myself somehow. Mixing chemicals was the only thing I learnt from my father, it was what I knew, I did petty jobs here and there to make a living and eventually I took myself through school. You'd expect me to hate the system and want revenge and all that, but I don't. I joined the British army where I served anti-bomb squad in Iraq. I served two tours in Iraq, in return, I needed something new, I needed a new adventure and one where I can use the gift I had so I joined the service and it's been that way ever since."

David sighed as he knew Josh had been through a lot, his personality was as a result of the battles he had fought, he could have turned out anyway, but he did the right thing. David wondered how much trouble it would have been if Josh had become an arsonist like his father or joined the crime bandwagon. They weren't the closest of friends but he sure was glad that Josh opted to join the service. David gulped what was left of his beer as he said to Josh, "In two days' time, you'd be taken to a secret bio-lab, belonging to the MI6, there we'd receive complete mission briefing from the director of operations. I don't know why exactly but I'm glad you are on my team. I've got to go, my wife and childwould be troubled at my absence. See you there and be safe." David stood up, stretched his hand for a handshake and walked away as Josh looked at him.

CHAPTER FOURTEEN:
CERTAINTY

David spent the rest of the day and the next showering Carla and Kim with all the love he had in him, he stayed close always not wanting to bat an eye from their presence. The desire to have them within touching distance at all times steered from the uncertainty of the outcome of his mission. Laura and Mark weren't left out, he didn't miss any opportunity to tell them how important they had been in his life. Life had taken one set of parents and had replaced them almost immediately with a pair that knew their job description almost as well as the original. He bought gifts whenever he could and even when it wasn't necessary, he did. His actions oozed the idea that he planned to leave but when he would he hadn't said. Carla loved every second of the attention he was throwing at her, but her fear rested on the fact that he was leaving. She said nothing to her parents giving him the chance to do it himself.

David picked a perfect time to break the news to Laura and Mark, a task that seemed even harder than telling Carla and Kim. Mark had taught him to know that his duty in life was to his family first and work and other affinity came after. Mark knew he loved his family but there was something about David that he wasn't letting anyone in on. What that was, no one knew but they weren't people to invade his personal space. They had always believed he knew what he wanted and believed as well that he wanted what was best for their daughter. Mark always made David believe they were transparent, and if he valued their relationship, he would make himself just as transparent.

David knew that was the ABCs to having a family but his reason for having secrets he couldn't tell for their own safety. He had crossed powerful people in his lifetime and even though he had them locked up, his family needed to be oblivious of his actions as a person. Besides, he was bound by an oath to tell no one of his involvement with the secret service. It was a union similar to marriage which was bound by the phrase, "Till death do us part." He loved Carla as it was obvious, his early life sweetheart, he had made no mistake making her his wife. He loved and appreciated her parents for the role they had played in his life, but he had taken this oath even before he met any of them and he was a man that kept his promises.

Carla, David and Kim had returned from the park that Friday evening, the trio had decided to have warm cups of tea as the skies had decided to let down rain on all of London. They sat down on the dining table as Laura and Mark rushed in, drenched from being under the rain a short time. Just from the driveway to the front door, Carla rushed in to get towels to dry themselves up as Kim rushed over to them not bothered that they were soaked from being in the rain. David rushed over to them to take from them their wet coats which he took to the laundry room. It was a nice evening for family to spend together.

Carla came from the room with two thick towels that she tossed to each of her parents. The pair collected and started to dry themselves. At David's house, they had clothes that they could wear seeing as they spent the majority of time there looking over Carla. They went in to change into outfits warmer to protect them from the cold. They returned from the room and met David, Kim and Carla back at the dining table drinking hot tea and telling themselves stories. Laura rushed over to Kim's side showering her with kisses as the little one laughed times over. They joined the tea drinking up until David signalled Carla and she said to Kim, "Hey baby, let's go play with dollies, I'm in the mood to weave some dolls hairs, how about you?" Kim, excited, jumped off the dining chair and ran first for her room, Carla following just behind.

David looked at Mark first before moving his gaze to Laura, he didn't know where to start from or how he was going to tell them he was going away for a while and to where would he say he was going to. Mark could sense the anxiety in David's face, he hadn't heard his voice, but he could tell something was wrong. He asked, "What is the matter son?"

Laura joined in, "Yes David, what is the matter? You can tell us anything." David could commune with them on all matters but where was he going to start telling them he was going away from.

He cleared his throat, sat upright on his chair as he replied, "This is harder than you think, I don't know how to say this that'll make it any easier."

Mark was determined to make him more comfortable than he already was, "You can say it anyway you can, we'll process it, and if it isn't the message you are passing, then you can correct our faulty conclusions."

David sighed as he said, "I have to go away yet again and this time just like last time, I don't know when I'll be back. I have been off work for quite a while now since the incident at Larimer but going back, I was given this task and I have to accept it if I'm going to keep my job."

Laura looked away as she couldn't bear to hear him say he was leaving yet again. Mark began talking to him, "I reckon you drop the job then mate, look after your family. I have always made you understand that a man's dry is to his family, every other engagement comes second, you are not doing that son, you are putting work over your wife. What's so special about this job that you can't just drop it and get another?"

David had answers for the question, "They were by me when I couldn't work, they took care of my bills, they made sure I was fine and I could feed my family when I was injured, I can't just leave them now when I'm fine. This is my last job, I promise you and Laura that after this one, I will quit and I will do something with Carla, Kim and the baby around here, we will build a family based on honesty, trust and transparency but for now, you have to understand where my decision sterns from."

Laura still didn't like the idea, she kept quiet hoping Mark would somehow find a way to convince David from going but she was shocked to her bones when Mark sighed and said to David, "I insert he desire to give back to the people who helped you look out for your family and for that reason alone I won't stop you, that doesn't mean I support you going away from your family for whatever time you are going to take. Do your wife and child know that you are going away for an indefinite amount of time?" David nodded his head to gesture that he had told them of his supposed voyage. That Mark was in support didn't mean Laura was. She snarled at Mark clearly disgusted by the ease with which he was allowing David off the hook, but Mark would pacify her anger, "He had the right to provide for his family. He is not very young, he needs to understand himself that his place is right here by his wife and not out there. Money will provide but it won't provide it all. You will provide it all, money and love and care and encouragement and whatever she needs. I have to remind you of one thing however, Laura and I won't always be here to look after Carla. Remember that once upon a time, your parents would be here right now on this table with your father almost whooping your ass if you say you are leaving but now, they are not here with us God bless their souls. The same fate will befall Laura and myself and then the question you'd ask yourself is have you learnt where you are supposed to be because if you haven't, you'd hurt your wife and your

s."

Mark was making sense, and Laura had every reason to scream her head off at his decision. They had every right to be angry at him, and Carla had every reason to divorce him and stay away from him. If only they knew why he was going, maybe they'd understand his point of view, he wouldn't have to work so hard in hiding his movement if he could tell Carla the sort of job that he did and why he had to go away so much. It was better when he had his nervous breakdown, he was always here even though his marriage was on the brink of collapse. He had discovered that it was impossible for him to create a balance between his job and his family. Mark called out for Carla who came to join up with them shortly after, he looked at Carla and made sure David saw him looking at Carla carefully, then he moved his eyes back to

David, creating the impression that he wanted David to notice something, and David could pick up the cryptic message. Mark wanted David to realize his wife was heavily pregnant and would be due in a couple of weeks. When Mark was sure David had picked up on the message, he asked Carla to sit as he continued talking, "I reckon you see the condition of your wife? I reckon you know that in no distant time, she'll be in labor? I reckon you know that when she goes to labor, you have to be there? I reckon you know that after she delivers your baby, you have to be there with her raising the baby together?" David nodded his head positively.

Mark continued, "These are the questions that you should ask yourself, are you ready to be a father? Even if you are ready, do you think you make a good father? If not, what are you doing to change that? You have told your wife about your supposed traveling, and she agreed but did you take a long hard look at her to see if she said that because she wanted to or she said it just so you'd be happy? Don't lose what others are searching for chasing after what you can clearly do without." He finished talking and gestured for Laura to stand up so they could make their leave.

This wasn't how David planned the night to be but he had lost control of the situation. He tried to calm Mark down, to sit so they could talk about this like men but Mark wouldn't have it. Mark looked at him, disappointed at his decision making, "I'm not angry at you, I just want you to have this conversation with your wife again, this time with you having an idea of how she'd feel if you stood up and left her to have your baby alone." David watched Laura and Mark leave the house despite the rain, he looked at Carla who sat before him with an expression that suggested he had a lot of convincing to do yet again.

Unsure what to say to Carla whom he thought he had convinced about the need to embark on the journey, David clenched to her fist tightly as he said to her, "I know I hurt you every time I pick up my bags and head for that door but this, I promise will be the last time. When I return, it'd be you and me and our children forever, I'll never leave again, I promise." Carla had no intention of forcing him to stay, she had hoped having his childwould be enough to keep him by her side forever and she had seen in his eyes the love he had for Kim.

She knew if he still insisted on going then he really had to go, she smiled as she said to him, "Don't worry about me, I'm not sad, I understand that you have to go but I'll be right here waiting for you, but promise me one thing yet again, that you'd return to me like you did the last time."

He held her fist still as he nodded his head, he stood up from his chair as he moved his face closer to hers. He let go of her hand as he moved his right hand to her face, stroking the hair that stood on her face to the side of her head, he fixed his gaze directly into her eyes. He moved his head towards hers as she closed her eyes, he leaned in and kissed her gently on the lips for a few minutes. He removed his lips and asked her, "Where is Kim?"

"She's asleep."

It felt like music to his ears that his little girl was asleep as he leaned forward again, kissing Carla repeatedly. She returned the favour as the pair stayed locked in each other's warm embrace and lips locked on a chilly night. Despite the emotions that ran through the room prior, David and Carla made sweet love like they had not in a while and both passed the night on the couch. As David let himself wonder into the warm embrace of his tiredness on a cold night, his thought came crawling. His mind drove straight into the possible outcome of his mission against ISIS. He remembered Saudi

Arabia and Russia with the success he obtained from both giving him renewed hope that he and his team would triumph over the current obstacle that stood in his way. He laid there in his thoughts for a while as Carla held him tightly even as she slept, there was no need trying to free from her firm grip, he'd be without his wife for an extended period that he wasn't even sure of so he might as well just enjoy this one.

CHAPTER FIFTEEN:
DEPARTURE

The next day went by, it was an awfully quiet day as neither David nor Carla wanted to talk about his going. They had their meals together the entire day each just trying to be positive. David did his best to reaffirm his love to his wife and his commitment to his family. Carla did not understand but her level of understanding that had made David love her from the beginning was still with her. She never liked it, but he never challenged his decision.

David had informed the Prime Minister of his team and had given coordinates for all the members of said team, they would be brought in for briefing by MI6 operatives as even David didn't know where the briefing would take place. He stayed in all day trying to gather what memories he could with Carla and Kim. The trio tried to make the day memorable, but the attempts were foiled by the often reminder that he was going away, and they weren't sure for how long.

It was almost five p.m. and he had to take them to Mark and Laura's. He wasn't sure how they'd receive him, but he had to. They boarded his vehicle as they drove down to Carla's parents. He drove quietly as Kim wondered why the sudden silence since the day started, she was an observant childbut saw sadness in Carla's eyes and said nothing. David dropped them off at her parents, Laura received them at the door and wouldn't make eye contact with David, he knew she was angry still. He tried to talk to her but she would have nothing of him, he walked into the house where he met Mark fixing the sink. He walked towards Mark, not sure how he'd treat him, but Mark had no ill feeling, Mark walked to him, and shook his hand, "I have no problem with you David, if you have convinced your wife that you have to go and she allowed you, I have no problems. She is my daughter after all and the more time she spends with me, the happy I am that I get to see my little girl. I just hope you know what you are doing. Get back in time and be with your family, I'm supposed to be enjoying my retirement with my wife and not babysitting yours and your child."

David had a smile on his face as he leaned in and hugged Mark, he stayed there for a few minutes before eventually letting go, he said, "I hope Laura forgives me, I have to do this, I promise it won't happen again." He went straight for Carla whom he kissed passionately before bending down on his knee and hugging Kim tightly. He kissed her as well on her forehead as he stood up and made for the door. Laura stood in her kitchen as she looked at him from afar, not wanting to say or do anything with him.

He was headed for the door but thought about his actions, he could not leave with Laura mad at him, she was his mother and he'd have a clearer head of everyone was happy with him. He went into the kitchen, she looked away like a toddler refusing her mother but he hugged her from behind as he whispered words into her ears, she smiled as she turned facing him and hugged him closely as tears dropped down her cheeks, she said to him, "You best be back before she had that baby else I'll kill you myself," he nodded as he headed for the car, he wasn't going until morning but he didn't know when they'd come for him so he had to be prepared for whenever MI6 operatives would pick him up.

The drive back home was quiet, literally because he had nobody to talk to, as he drove back, he thought of what he was to expect. He was still deep in thought when his phone rang, it was the Prime Minister on the special line that he had to connect with the political leader of Britain. The Prime Minister sounded optimistic about the mission that was about to start, "Son, I have been trying to get to you for a while now, but I haven't been able to, where have you been? There's an update in the case and I'm sure it's one you'd like."

"What is this update you speak of sir?"

The Prime Minister couldn't contain his joy as he continued speaking, "We have our hands on one of the ISIS operatives, he was apprehended yesterday at a raid by metropolitan police earlier today. ISIS had a shopping mall factory around Fulham, it was a regular apartment, but they had there a weapons store. We got an anonymous tip about excessive activities going on around the house and the police raided the place with all suspects. They were already clearing out as we couldn't find anything useful but him."

"That's good news sir, has he said anything to interrogators?"

The Prime Minister continued, "He hasn't said anything to anyone. He had refused to spill but we are still hoping we could get him to talk. I requested to be kept abreast about all proceedings of this mission because I want to know daily how it goes. The fate of Britain rests on you successfully solving this problem and I trust you will never let us down."

David smiled gently, "Thank you sir for the news, he will, whether he likes it or not, lead us to the other members of his team. The house in Fulham, we are going to need to look it up. There might be something else that we'll find there. I need forensics on the scene sir, can that be done?" It wasn't normal, but David was giving orders to the Prime Minister. That was how much the Prime Minister had placed his faith on David.

He dropped the call as he continued his quiet drive home, his house even quieter, the idea that he'd be without his family hit different as he walked into the empty apartment. He took a glass of vodka, laid back as he slept off. His heart and mind already in the field while his body laid asleep. This was definitely his last rodeo but what was he to expect from this very outing. Even he wasn't sure but it's part of the job. The uncertainty gives it the thrill that they crave.

CHAPTER SIXTEEN:
MISSION BRIEFING

David woke up as early as four a.m., he had barely slept, he was in and out of sleep, and the anxiety of beginning one of the biggest missions of his entire career had the better of him. He washed his mouth and turned on the TV, he sat on the couch with a bowl of cereal waiting for the pickup. His phone rang and when he picked up, it was Sarah, apparently, he wasn't the only one who had been nervous, she had barely slept as she began talking, "Good morning Dave.

Today is the big day. I had barely slept the last two days, wanting to begin the mission. This isn't my line of work, but I want to thank you yet again for giving me the chance to serve my country in this capacity. I'm not going to let you down. When do we leave?" David could hear from her voice the extent of her anxiety and he couldn't blame her, she was used to the military pattern of breaking in and solving issues with guns and fists and boots but this time, she was going to be working with spies who'd rather they experience no confrontation. It was a different scenery from what she understood. Her selection was a huge gamble, but he had his reasons, and he was not one to regret his actions.

He tried to calm her down, "Sarah, it's okay, you don't have to panic, this will be like a walk in the park, and we are going to get through this with no complications. As for our ETA, even I don't know that, the MI6 agents will come get you when the time is right, just go with them and we'll meet wherever it is they are taking you. It's going to be alright." Hearing his voice gave her a sense of calm as she accepted and dropped the call. The blanket of nightfall had given way to sunrise, it was still dark and silent outside when David Heard a car pullover in his driveway. He held on to his bag as he heard knocks on his door. He walked to the door where he met four men dressed in black suits, none with any expression on their faces, they covered his head with a bag as they took him into the car.

He wondered why they went through all the stress. He wasn't going to tell anyone where he had been, even if they had a gun to his head, but it was protocol not to let him in on the location of secret bases. David sat still in between two men as the car drove away from his home. They were on the road for over thirty minutes before making a stop, he was brought down, the bag still over his head. He heard muffled sounds around him like someone else had been brought to the site. He smiled knowing it could be a member of his team, he made no sound and offered no resistance. The duffle bag removed from his head, he was in the middle of nowhere. It was still dark, but the location made it darker, the trees stood tall, broad hiding the building that stood behind, he walked gently as he saw a building standing on its own in the middle of nowhere.

He was not sure what route he took to get here but he understood that whatever happens here was secret and need not be seen by anybody. He looked around him seeing each member of his team standing in between two men dressed in suits. They were led into the building which ordinarily was just a good old fashion apartment, decorated to meet the taste of an exquisite architect, the furniture crafted to perfection and the house arranged in such a way that even the greatest artists would appreciate its symmetry. They followed the men not making sounds, not even acknowledging that they knew each other. Not long, they approached the fireplace with a moose head hanging just over the fire.

One of the men tilted one of the horns on the moose and they heard a sound like a door was unlocked, the frame of the fireplace moved forward as a door appeared out of nowhere, the door slid opened and the four of them were ushered in with the men staying behind. Before the door shut itself completely, one of the men leaned in and pressed a button just by the door, the compartment was an elevator and it was headed down. They kept quiet as it moved gently a floor or two into the ground.

The door opened, they saw an office space that looked as though it were midday. The place filled with people that went about that duty like they didn't even exist. None stopped to talk or ask who they were, it was like they had been expecting them. David walked out of the elevator into the office, he was about to start asking questions when a lady walked up to him, "You must be David Scarlet, I'm Jessica Hayden, you can come with me." She turned around as she walked straight into a hallway that had many office doors, she headed for the very last office, which read on the door, Director Ashley Barnes.

Powers had changed hands in the service and David hadn't met with the current director. He walked into the office after which his teammates followed but the lady didn't, she locked the door behind them as she walked away. The man stood up from his seat, he walked towards David as he stretched out his hand for a handshake, a gesture which he repeated for the rest of the team. After he was done, he walked towards a door in his office and asked David and the others to follow, it was a conference room with seats and a screen.

He walked in and right there in front of the seats, the Prime Minister was seated, he looked like one who had not slept for a while. His skin was pale, his hair unkempt and his eyes had sunk in with dark circles around them, he wasn't taking this invasion thing easily David thought. The four of them stood not moving an inch as no order had been given. The Prime Minister, lost in his own thoughts, was called by the director. David saw a shell of the man he had been friends with a while, he was letting the pressure of the terrorist organization take the better of him. He wondered why because the last time they spoke, he sounded happy so how did he get here?

Ashley Barnes asked them to sit down, he started talking when the Prime Minister interrupted, "I will do it, let me do it." Ashley nodded his head as he took his seat on the chair that stood facing David and his teammates. The Prime Minister started his briefing, "I reckon you know why you are here, but if you don't, I will tell you. You have been selected to be part of a tactical team that has been designated to free Britain from the siege of a terrorist organization that calls itself the ISIS. Some weeks ago, the Larimer Square shopping mall was attacked, thanks to one of you here, the casualties were reduced but while we focused on the attack at Larimer Square, the terrorists took us by surprise storming our secret research facility. They didn't go there on a hunch, they went there with information on what was inside and they didn't take anything else save for one thing, The Declon 5 nerve agent. In front of you all, there are files containing everything you need to know about the chemical."

There was silence as he gave them time to go through the contents of the file, they read it for a few minutes before he continued talking, "Now, according to David's account on the Larimer Square shopping mall incident, he said that the leader of the group chanted *ISIS Forever* just before he blew himself up and other members of his team. We got a call a day after the attack at Larimer Square shopping mall, a man with a heavily accented voice claimed responsibility for the attack. We hadn't noticed that the chemical was gone until they mentioned it themselves." The team murmured as the Prime Minister paused to adjust his shirt before he continued talking, "I know this is bonkers as no one should have access to this lab or vault to take something of importance but that is not the issue we came here to discuss. We accept that it was a lapse on our part and we have moved on and that is why you are here. Declon 5 is dangerous, if used wrongly, it can put us in a dangerous situation and that is why we want you to retrieve it. At first we thought mass producing it would be impossible because we assumed that the notes of its formation was still intact but I was told we had experimented on it and had saved the information of its process in a drive and backed it into the system right here in this bio-lab and unfortunately for us, that was stolen as well. We'd had thought nothing of it but members of ISIS contacted Downing Street, the queen is a frenzy at the moment and has demanded that we retrieve the Declon 5 and its missing files whatever way possible."

David had questions but it didn't seem like it was time to ask them, the Prime Minister continued, "Declon 5 is truly dangerous, and for a city like London and a country like Britain, it could be really devastating. I'm sure you've gone through the files before you, it can be infused into the city's central water system or made into a dirty bomb and either way, it'd cause too much damage. The organization contacted us a while back and gave us a month to decide to her terms else she will bring Britain to her knees."

David cut in at this point, "What are her terms?"

The Prime Minister had been trying his best to avoid that question, he hesitated in responding, creating the impression that ISIS's demands were something that might be just. Regardless, threatening the lives of millions of English men and women was no way to sort diplomatic issues, diplomacy was the way, but diplomacy was already out of the window. Its boat had sailed hence the need for ISIS to take drastic measures.

David pushed further with his question, "I know our job doesn't permit us to ask questions, but humanity demands we do, I hope we aren't doing anything that might compromise our stand in ensuring world peace?"

The Prime Minister cut in immediately, "I assure you, David, Britain hasn't done anything to warrant the siege at Larimer Square shopping mall and the threat she's getting. The operations of ISIS although young had spread across the shores of major European powers and even I to America.

The group is getting worldwide recognition at the expense of innocent lives. I'm sure you know that whatever it is they are fighting for, killing innocent people is never the way to speak up. When we neutralize the threat, we might hearken to their plea and review their stand, but the immediate move is to ensure Britain is safe and her citizens secured. Understood?"

David wasn't through with his question, he asked, "What does ISIS have to do with the Russians? At Larimer Square, all the terrorists I encountered were Russians, their names and accent gave them away. Are they involved in this yet again?"

Sarah jumped in, "I noticed it as well, the two I neutralized had heavy Russian accents and called themselves by European names, Russian, Ukrainian, Polish, I couldn't tell but I knew it was European." The Prime Minister pulled a shopping mall remote from the table in front of him as he pointed it to the table and pressed a button, the screen displayed a picture of a man with tattoos all over his face running down into his neck. "There isn't much about ISIS out there but the most we have is that this man out here Igor Krishikov is the one making the calls for the group, he is the only one whose face remains open whenever they make these video calls and make demands. We've made contact to the Russian government laying aside previous grievances to give us all they can about him, but it seems he never existed, all efforts to locate him from all countries in the world have proven unsuccessful. He is the base of your mission, locate him and we can be close to solving our problems."

Roger, looking keenly at the screen, asked the Prime Minister, "If with all the resources at your disposal, you haven't been able to find him, what are the odds that we will find him given that there's just five of us?"

The Prime Minister sat down on the table as he drank from his bottle of water, he sighed as he sort to give answer to the question just asked, "I don't know whatever methods you want to make us of but on grounds of resources, know this, whatever data belonging to the government of Britain that you wish to access would be made available. This is a matter of national security and is a priority and will be treated as such."

He stood up from the table as he walked towards the screen yet again, he pushed the button and a map appeared. It was some almost destroyed particle laying on the table, he looked at it and looked back at them, "There's still a lot that needs to be said, the material you see on the screen is an explosive but I don't know anything about explosives so I'm going to let Captain Jack Sawyer fill you in on what it is and what we think of it."

The five of them looked around for the captain when a man well over six feet walked into the room, he had broad shoulders, a scar across his right eye. His right eyeball dead as was his soul, he spoke like he had seen death many times and had no fear of it, he spoke lightly of every matter and made them know that he still had in him the desire to gear up and go back into the field to put an end to the menace. He had an aura about him that suggested he attended to matter like a brute believing too much in the application of brute force. As he walked in, the Prime Minister introduced him, "Ladies and gentlemen, Captain Jack Sawyer of the British Special Forces anti-bomb squad."

He received the introduction and greeting as though it was completely unnecessary, he looked at them thoroughly before saying anything, "I have no need for time wasting, what you see on the screen is a bomb, it's a covered bomb and studying the constituents of the bomb, my men discovered that it was RDX, which is a nitrogen explosive, it's misinformation having the presences of numerous nitrogen-nitrogen bonds without the presence of oxygen, norshopping mally nitrogen bonds try to come together to form nitrogen gas which is very potent. The more the nitrogen-nitrogen bonds, the more powerful the bomb would be and judging from the explosion at Larimer Square, this was really potent."

Josh McGee enjoyed this part of the conversation as he listened with joy, the captain looked at him, not understanding why the mention of explosions was giving him a sick fix. He walked straight to Josh, "You like explosives?" Josh nodded his head, the captain smiled, "Then I believe you know the implication of RDX explosives?"

Josh nodded his head as the captain gave him the chance to explain what an RDX bomb meant to their case, he stood up as he explained loudly, "RDX are explosives used by Russian Special Forces, it is not trademark to any other force and is sometimes really difficult to deactivate, but luckily for us, I have spent hours exposed to

RDX explosives without protection just so I could deactivate it under pressure, and funny enough, it's not the hardest bomb to deactivate."

The captain thought he had seen it all, but Josh was different, as he walked away, he said to Josh, "Should you make it out of this alive, see me, we have a lot to talk about."

The Prime Minister thanked Sawyer as he left the from, he turned back to David, "To your question of Russian involvement, we are not sure what part they play in all this but we are certain now that whoever makes the bomb is ex Special Forces, he could still be in active service, we aren't sure but he's Russian. We also studied the plastic that housed the bomb, its normal plastic but hardened differently. Norshopping mally you'd use biphenyl to harden plastic but that wasn't the usual biphenyl, something else was added, the scientists called it BCP and guess what region BCP is mass produced? It might not be Russia but it is close, it is in

Ukraine, the shopping mall city of Zhovkva. We didn't leave you with nothing, you have a guide, and the rest is up to you to figure out what to do. Your mission starts tomorrow. My job isn't done but I believe I've done as much as I can. Do not hesitate to call me if you need anything, I believe it is obvious that David is in charge. God speed lads."

CHAPTER SEVENTEEN: DISPATCH

The briefing had come to an end, the Prime Minister and the director headed for the exit door, David signalled his team to wait behind but first he had things to find out. He followed after the Prime Minister into the hallway where he met him neck deep in conversation on his phone. David looked at him seriously suggesting he wasn't going away until he had been listened to, the

Prime Minister ended his call to give David the audience he craved, and he gestured to the director to give them the privacy David demanded.

He ushered David into a quiet office where the both of them sat down close to each other taking in hushed tones to avoid eavesdropping of any kind. David sounded serious as he wasn't placing his life and that of his teammates on chance, if he was going to address this then he needed all the information he could get on ISIS and the motive behind their attack was part of that information. He hadn't said anything, but the Prime Minister knew what he wanted. David leaned forward as he said as quiet as he could, "I know this isn't going to be easy for you talking about diplomatic issues above my pay check and all but I will need you to tell me what is going on, we can't go out there not knowing what we're looking at or looking for. Does the ISIS have a legitimate reason to attack Britain and other members of the European Union and what reason do they have spreading their operations beyond the shores of Europe?"

The Prime Minister sighed, this was going to be hard letting David in on, it was a matter reserved for heads of state but David was more than just an agent. He was a friend of the Prime Minister, he had advised him on many issues and that should count for something, the Prime Minister, his hand on the table said quietly to David, "There is a legitimate reason why ISIS is attacking us today but their methods are extreme. Recently, the European Union majorly of the United Kingdom, Germany, France, Netherlands, Russia and Belgium came together to work on a new invention, a non-traceable missile. This missile perfected could avoid radar and help win wars in single goes. It was being tested off the shores of Kazakhstan but there was an error, it had some technical difficulties and destroyed a village that stood nearby. The powers of the

EU found a way to sweep the matter under the rug. I don't know if that is the case, but ISIS has sworn revenge against European superpowers. During the video I had with the leader Igor Krishikov, he threatened to not rest until the powers that be taste similar fate to shopping maller nations like Kazakhstan. I know we are wrong but why should a lot of innocent people die for our mistakes?"

David, shocked at what he just heard continued speaking, "What happens if the leaders of the European countries involved in the missile testing openly apologize to the village involved and the people that lost their loved ones in the attack?"

The Prime Minister cut in, "We can't do that."

David didn't understand why, it could end all the tension that was growing in Britain and other European countries, "Why can't you sir? It's not a tough move to make, we apologize for our mistakes and everybody moves on."

The Prime Minister shook his head as he attempted to make David understand the politics behind the entire scenario. "We can't do that because the missile was not supposed to be made public. The idea was brought up to the UN by the EU of creating missiles that could avoid being tracked but it was rebuffed at the UN general meeting on grounds of being too excessive in the art of war. We didn't heed the warning and continued its creation. If words went out that we have a weapon of that magnitude, it would create tension among members of the G8 and G20 and it might plunge the world into a state of unrest. It will unsettle the world and put it on the edge, should anything go wrong from there, we could be witnessing a World War Three. We can't for any reason let the world know what happened in Kazakhstan."

Regardless of the situation, it didn't make sense to David why lives of the masses would be placed under risk just because they made a mistake and can't make an open apology. David looked at the Prime Minister, disappointed, "What happens to the lives of English men and women, are we going to put them at risk because of something you did? Does it not matter to you that countless numbers of people might die for something we can avoid by just coming out and trying to dialogue with the other continents on what you did and close the case somehow? Whatever happened to putting the lives of the masses before our very own? They are the ones you serve after all. I don't like what is going on let it be known but I agree with one thing, they are being extreme by threatening English lives so yes I'll try my best to stop them but please from here on out, try not to hide sensitive things as this from me, they'll be really useful in solving this case."

David stood up and headed for the door as the Prime Minister left for the bio-lab. David headed back for the briefing room where he met the rest of the team seated waiting for him, he said to them as he took his seat, "A lot has been said and we must have thought between ourselves. Other things need to be said but before I allow everybody to contribute, I just want to let you know that our mission has gone beyond the English border, it has spread to Ukraine and just recently to Kazakhstan, the boundaries of the operations of ISIS has spread reaching corners of Europe that we didn't think possible. Finding Igor Krishikov is key to solving the mysteries behind this group and I won't rest until I have found out who he is and why he has opted to bring pain to Britain and to Europe in general. This is going to be a team effort, I need all the help I can get so if you have any suggestion to this please speak up and help us out."

Josh jumped at the avenue, "I have something in mind. The protective plastic of the RDX bomb that was sampled a while ago, I know where the BCP is produced, I can't say it's the only source but it makes perfect sense as it is in Zhovkva, Ukraine. I didn't think much about it but after you left with the Prime Minister, I confirmed something that happened a while ago. I needed material some time ago to house unstable nitrogen and plutonium for a bomb I was building and the regular protective plastic couldn't hold it right? A friend of mine suggested I get BCP hardened protective cover and he said I could get it from stores here, but he knew where it was in mass production and it was Zhovkva. I know where we need to start, in Ukraine, if we can find the producer and identify to whom he had been selling to, we can start to locate the other missing pieces in the case."

David liked the suggestion, he waited a while for other opinions, but none was forthcoming, it looked slim but it was the lead they had, David stood up from his chair as he said, "Thanks Josh, we'll begin from there. First thing in the morning, Josh, Sarah and I will head for Ukraine to look into that, Andrew and Roger, you team up with other MI6 operatives, study evidence from the Larimer Square attack and pay attention to evidence that had been gathered earlier. Whenever we get back, we compare findings, and we move on from there. How's that?" There was no obstruction as everyone agreed to that plan. This was the beginning of not just a mission to save English lives but a mission to liberate those that were oppressed.

CHAPTER EIGHTEEN: PENULTIMATE

"We have to prepare ourselves to leave as early as we can, the deadline that handed Britain by ISIS is too close for comfort. Josh, I need information on the BCP producer and distributor ASAP, that's our target once we stop at Zhovkva. I know we were told that we have the resources of the English government at our disposal, but we need to be as discreet as we can, we can't afford to attract attention to ourselves. We make Zhovkva, meet up with him, get his client list one way or the other and make our way from there. Andrew, I leave you in charge of operations back here in London, I believe there is something that you'd see if you go through the rubbles of Larimer. We've all had blistering careers but right here is the defining moment. If we can't protect our home, it's as good as saying we didn't exist. I take it we are all prepared for what comes next? Because whatever comes next defines us," David charged the team as he made for the exit, "You can see yourself to the quarters, if you can't, there'll be agents waiting to show you to your quarters."

As he headed for the door, Josh stopped him, "One step ahead of you Cap, the name of the BCP producer is Lukasz Cherishev. He runs local production, not with any recognized company or what not, he is the sort of man that could be behind productions of this nature. While you spoke, I was able to get all the information I could on our man, he is said to run a shopping mall factory in his building in Lwow district in Zhovkva. He has managed to keep a really low profile, but I believe we can get him and that would kick start of reaction. Pardon me for not listening throughout your briefing but I'm a kind of guy that goes with the flow."

David laughed as he stood, the frame of the door in his hand, he said, "I can feel assured knowing that we aren't walking into Ukraine blind, we have a target, and our target is to get Cherishev. Go get yourself some rest lads, you need it." He walked away as every one of them left the briefing room, it really was going to be a tough road ahead, but David was confident in the ability of his team, he was sure of the men he had picked and knew it'd be alright.

David got to his quarters, he laid on his bed, unable to sleep, he looked upwards. His vision beholding the walls but his thoughts beholding possibilities, he was unsure how this mission would go. He had promised his entire team that he'd guarantee their safety, but it wasn't in his hand, the very first turn of the mission had them parting ways. He was going to be in hostile territory but those he was leaving behind in Britain weren't exactly safe, he reached for his phone, they had retrieved his phone and that of his teammates and had given them devices that couldn't be tracked, he hadn't any calls, but he wasn't expecting any as Carla didn't have this number. He scrolled through the phone and the only information he had on the phone was Carla's number. They had permitted them one call to one person, and they didn't even get to decide who it'd be.

He contacted Carla who picked up in a hurry like she was expecting a call, "Hello, who is this?"

David kept quiet for a second, "Hey babe, it's David, how are you? How's Kim?"

Carla sounded like she was about to cry, she gasped for breath before she replied, "We are fine, I experienced a little setback today but thanks to Kim, I swear she acts like a grown up sometimes and I wonder just how mature she is."

David cut in, "Setback? What do you mean by setback? Are you sure you are okay?"

She laughed a little, "It's nothing, I just started feeling some pains in my abdomen, it got so intense I could barely stand, I started to feel dizzy, Kim walked in, saw me on the floor and alerted the neighbours. I'm really happy I have her around. Over to you honey, do you know when you'd return now?"

David sighed, he was happy she was fine but had no clue when he'd return, he said, "You shouldn't stress yourself too much Carla, I never thought having our own baby would bring this much discomfort to you, if I had, I wouldn't have pushed for it this bad, I'm sorry."

Carla laughed, "I don't mind doing this for us, it's only for now, in no distant time, I'll have the baby and we'll both forget about all this suffering and I'm eternally grateful that you brought Carla to our lives, she's an angel in a child's body."

David was comfortable knowing Carla had grown fond of Kim, "How's Kim and your parents?

"They are fine, it's not been easy without you here, but they are doing their best and

I'm fine, we all are. I miss you David and I can't wait to have you back."

David sighed, "Carla, I don't know when I'll be back yet, I know I hurt you every time I leave you for weeks but I want you to know that as I promised, this will be the very last time. Once I make it back home, I won't go again, ever again, it'll be me, you and Kim for the rest of our lives. I promise you and I will make it up to you." Carla accepted the offer, the pair spent the next few minutes talking about different things. David savoured the moment because he couldn't tell when it'd happen again. Carla wasn't willing to let go of him because she knew it'd be a while for him to communicate with her. His last departure was still fresh in her memories, she loved her husband a lot. Her only plan in life was to spend life with him.

David ended the call eventually and was back to his abyss of thoughts, Carla was no longer on the other end and reality was staring down at him. With Carla, he had forgotten what sat in front of him. She always took away his worries and made him believe that with her by his side, he had nothing to worry about. He had his eyes fixed at the wall, he could do with a glass of wine but he had no means of getting any. He stood up from his bed, trying to get some air to clear his head, he headed for the window and just as he walked, he heard a knock on his door, it was gentle. Whoever it was didn't want to alert anyone. He headed straight for the door and before him was Sarah.

There was silence between them for a few seconds as she tried to explain what she was doing there, he hadn't ushered her in as they both just stood there staring deeply at each other, David broke the silence when he asked her, "What is the problem, Sarah? Why aren't you asleep?"

She looked at him right back, "Why aren't you?"

He laughed a little as he moved from the door to allow her in, he had a million reasons why he wasn't asleep but he didn't feel he needed to explain anything to her, "You came to my quarters so if anybody has to explain themselves, it has to be you, I was just going to bed anyways before I heard you walk."

Sarah sat down on the chair that stood just by the table, she had on her an expression that she was concerned about the outcome of the mission that began in the morning. David looked at her, he could see her worry, this wasn't her type of operation, he understood. "I am worried David and it's not just because I've been out of service for a while, it's because of what happened to the teams I served in."

"What do you mean?"

She cleared her throat as she sat upright, leaning towards David. She found it difficult to say the words as she didn't know how he would receive it, she mustered the courage and said it as best she could, "I have been with two squadrons during my service and it was fun at first but they met their end really fast. I don't know but I feel my presence in a team is bad luck, I know I'm not supposed to think that way but why have I been the one to make it from the ill-fated end of both teams? Why didn't I die like the rest of them? I'm not better than them so why not then?"

David walked close to her as he patted her on the shoulder, he placed his hand on her jaw as he carried her head up so she could look into his eyes and her his, he said to her in the most gentle tone ever, "It's the pressure speaking, that you lost your teams in battle doesn't mean you are jinxed or you were the cause, it meant it was supposed to happen. Don't think of it that they died prematurely, think of it that they died serving their country, that they died protecting those they loved and some they didn't even know, don't see them as dead, see them as externals whose spirit and passion and fire burns within you and me and every other person out there looking to protect their countries and their families. You don't have to worry about that. I'm not ready to die yet and I can say the same about every other person in our team, you inclusive. We've all stood in the door of death, more times than we can count and every time, we walk through unscathed, it'll be the same this time as well, I promised you I'd bring you all back home safe and I keep my promises."

Sarah felt a surge of confidence shoot through her, she stood up from the chair, she had received what she came for but as she left, she looked back at David and said, "This might be my first time working with you but I'm sure it'd be the best outing I've ever been on, thanks for the confidence. Oh and if there ever comes a time where you have to pick between saving me and yourself, please save yourself and leave me behind. You have a family to take care of and I have no one, I have the belief that I am living on borrowed time, don't tell me because you promised me you'll bring me back home. You make the decision of sacrificing yourself for me, you are a natural born leader and the service will need your expertise for years to come but I'm replaceable. I don't need you to answer, I just wanted you to know how I feel."

David had a response, but he let her walk away and said nothing, he had seen all too well friends die in the field. Saudi Arabia and Tver, he knew the feeling and he was not ready to let it happen, not again, he'd give his life a time over if he was faced with the situation. She might think she has no one and wasn't valuable to life but he believed in her abilities from Larimer that he had met her, he knew why she didn't die in those attacks at Afghanistan and Iraq, it was because she had skills, it was no fluke, her potentials and he wasn't going to let her die and let it go to waste.

He smiled as he watched her walk away, he went to the window and opened it, breeze entered into the room, rippling through his hair, the smell of nature's fragrance had found its way into the room. David stood by the window a while absorbing nature in its purest form, after ten minutes of standing, he laid down on the bed, he wanted to drift into his thoughts but nature's call was upon him, he fell asleep a few minutes later. He fell asleep thinking of his end, he wondered how he'd die but his subconscious interrupted those thoughts. Maybe, just maybe, it wasn't his time to go, he still had fight left in him and he was going to keep fighting.

CHAPTER NINETEEN:
ZHOVKVA

The night passed quickly as David finally found solace in the peace that sleep brought upon him, but it was short lived, his alarm buzzer brought him back to reality at exactly four a.m. It was the day that it all began, the MI6 had ensured that they had three tickets for L'viv International Airport in Ukraine, just 23.2 km away from the town of Zhovkva. David got up as he got prepared, his thoughts still pondered on possible outcomes, the risks were obvious but not trying posed even more risks than trying. He was ready in next to no time, he went into the hallway where he met Sarah and Josh just in front of their door, nobody said anything for a few seconds until David broke the silence, "Good morning, I hope you are ready because today marks the beginning of the next few weeks." They replied as he picked up his bag and headed for the driveway, they did the same and followed him carefully.

Outside at the driveway, there were three vehicles, none that stood out more than usual, he had a Volkswagen Golf, Josh a Ford Focus and Sarah a Ford Fiesta. They all had drivers seated in their respective driver's seat as they sat on the passengers' seat. It was in a bid to be natural, for all they knew, ISIS could have an inside man, it was a possibility that David never ruled out, that they could infiltrate a secret bio-lab that had tight security, they'd have gotten Intel from someone who had ideas of how the base worked. They needed not attract too much attention to themselves. While in the car, their plane tickets were handed to them as the cars drove away.

The drive to London City Airport wasn't a long one, the bio-lab was in London the whole time, it wasn't far off from Downing and the airport itself, how something so secured was infiltrated still was a mystery to David but solving this case would reveal so many mysteries to David and his team. The flight was scheduled for six a.m., it was a three-hour flight to L'viv Airport and an hour drive to Lwow. It was as scheduled, the flight and the arrival, nothing out of the ordinary had happened to David for a while and he had hoped for his own sake that it would continue that way.

They arrived at L'viv at around nine forty-five a.m., the town was shopping mall, it was mostly natural, the trees kissed the sky as the mountains at the edges of the city stood tall, It had shopping mall buildings as it boasted a shopping mall population, and one could count by fingers the people that stood at a place in time. It looked a city that had seen neither difficult times nor wars. Coming out of the airport, David beheld the city as he walked out of the airport. It wasn't much in terms of structures, but it had in itself, natural scenery that captivated the eyes. The trio boarded a taxi that was headed their way, Josh had the coordinates needed to find Lukazs Cherishev. It was a simple matter of getting there. They had to be as discreet as they could if they were going to come in and out of Ukraine without attracting attention to themselves.

Thirty minutes later, they were at Lwow, the address that Josh had produced, a shabby apartment that looked like it hadn't seen care in over a decade. The walls had cracks that had become so obvious, there were holes seen from the outside that the building was already gone. As David beheld the structure, his memories ran back to the hideout he shared with Harold at Litvinski during his mission at Tver in Russia. He was determined this time to ensure the outcome of this mission differs from that one.

As they approached the door, a stench halted them, it smelled so foul, they had to cover their nostrils, David looked at Josh and in a hushed tone, he asked him, "Are you sure this is the place where the hardened protective covers are made?"

Josh raised both his shoulders. Sarah cut in, "Are we going to focus on the quality of the building and not the smell that we can perceive?" She got no response as they stood before the door, David tried to open the door and without struggle, it opened like it wasn't even locked.

Contrary to the look of the house from outside, it was neatly arranged inside, the chairs were set as the TV was on, and there were two cups of coffee on the table. "Something doesn't feel right here, it looks like someone was here recently and what is that smell?" David said. He gestured his index fingers of both hands gesturing that Sarah should search through the kitchen and Josh through the room by the side while he made his way through the dining room. Something seemed ominous about the building, and he was desperate to find out.

For every step taken, the building would wreak extremely loud, the very foundations were beginning to give way, the stench filled the air, it's foul odour moved around chasing anybody that dared come close. They tried to pay attention to the smell to see if they'd find what its cause was. The house was tidy and empty, save for the TV that was on, nothing around the apartment made it look like someone had been there a while. The sounds of the floor increased as Sarah walked towards the room, she placed her feet on a certain spot and the sound was different from every other place she had stepped on, something was underneath that spot. She called for David and Josh, "I think I found something."

They rushed to her side, moving from that spot a shopping mall rug that rested on the floor, beneath it was a shopping mall door. David pulled it open and it felt like they had just opened a cage for a wild beast as the smell escaped through the shopping mall door. David covered his nostril with his left hand as he picked up a knife from the kitchen counter, they walked in one after the other, starting with David, Josh just behind and Sarah coming in last. As they went in, the smell worsened, it was dark, David in his blinded state searched the place for a switch until he found a rope dangling from the floor of the house which doubled as the roof of the basement. He pulled it and a shopping mall bulb lit up, it hardly illuminated the place, but it was more than they needed.

The smell wasn't as bad when they initially entered the house or their nostrils as well as their lungs had gotten used to the smell. Making their way to the point of its origin had reduced the effect the stench had on them, the basement looked like a lab of some sort with barrels lying idle on the floor in their numbers. David held his knife firmly, the house looked quiet, but he had witnessed no ills from being extra careful. He walked slowly and carefully, opening the first barrel and finding it filled with a slimy liquid that clearly was the cause of the foul stench that filled the building. He picked up a stick which had the chemical residue all over it, it must be what the scientist mixes his chemical with, and he placed it into the barrel down to the floor of the barrel hoping to find something, anything that would lead them to the whereabouts of whoever lived in the apartment.

He did the same for all the barrels that stood on the floor but there was nothing in any of the barrels. He kept the stick as they all continued canvassing through the basement for signs of life, but they could find nothing save the rats that ran through the place. David looked at Josh as he said, "Are you sure this is the place?" Josh nodded his head positively as they continued their search. They looked around but nothing was found. Sarah had climbed out of the basement and was still searching around the main house, she walked towards the kitchen and looked through the kitchen door and saw a shopping mall shaft that stood a few meters away from the house. The house stood on a property that had barely been used, behind the house was so much space, it had trees covering the shed probably as a means to keep out prying eyes.

Sarah called out for David and Josh again, who rushed out to see what she was calling them for, they went straight out of the building hoping they'd find some answers in the shed knowing fully well that they had to find Cherishev. They followed the path that led them to the shed. A shopping mall bulb was on in the building and as they walked in, David saw a shadow cover the illumination from the bulb for a few seconds like something or someone had run across the bulb but he placed no thoughts to it. He took charge as he said to Sarah and Josh as quiet as he could be, "There's someone around, I felt it, it's probably Cherishev who is a little careful but be careful." He walked towards the door of the shed, with Sarah and Josh on one side of the door and him on the other, his knife was still in his hand, they had no guns with them and needed to avoid confrontation as much as possible. He pushed the door open, and this time, there was no smell.

They walked in, searching the entire place. Josh signalled to David as he saw a shopping mall office that stood just on one corner of the shed, he rushed there as Sarah continued to look around the shed. When David arrived at the office door, he tried to open it but it was closed, he tried to force it but to no avail, it wasn't opening. Josh gestured to him to give him a little space, he bent down and brought out a shopping mall pin from his breast pocket, he placed the pin into the lock, manipulating the lock for a few seconds after which the door was unlocked. He opened the door and before them was a corpse, Josh brought out a photo and looked at it before looking at the man sitting there on his table with bullet holes in his chest, abdomen and forehead.

They walked towards the corpse, David felt it, "It's warm, whoever killed him either just left here or is still somewhere inside as we speak." As they stood analysing the body, Sarah let out a shout. They rushed out to see a man dressed in a hood covering his head, he had Sarah in a hole with his hands over her throat attempting to suffocate her. When he saw them approach, he left her on the floor and fled. Sarah laid on the floor trying to catch her breath, David said to Josh as he made chase, "Tend to her, I will go after him." Josh obliged and stopped by Sarah to see if she had sustained any injuries while David chased after the suspect.

The man ran into the woods avoiding every obstacle that stood in his way, David chased after him not so fortunate to avoid every obstacle that came his way. His heart throbbing as he ran through the woods, his breath came fast, his feet making stumping sounds as he made his way through the woods. He wasn't familiar with the terrain, and he found it difficult to avoid all that stood in his way, he could barely keep up with the man who seemed to be in his twenties and had enough energy to run away from the grasp of David who stopped after running a short while. Disappointed, he went back to see how Sarah was.

As he ran back, the only thing that came to his mind was that he promised Sarah he'd take her back home alive and unhurt and at the very first taste of action, she had already been injured. He got back and she was seated on the chair, he rushed to her side trying to be sure she was fine, to his greatest surprise, she wasn't downhearted at all, she brought out a wallet from her pocket as both stood there surprised at what she was doing, she handed the card over to David as she said, "I pulled the wallet off the guy that just ran away, he jumped me from behind, pushed me down and mounted me in a bid to suffocate me, I owe you guys my life." David still wasn't convinced she was fine, he dropped the card on the floor as he checked her thoroughly to be sure she was fine.

When certain that she was okay, he collected the wallet, looking through it, he found an identification card, some notes of money amounting to just over a hundred hryvnia, he accessed the card, and on it, he saw the name Andriy Kilitchsko. He smiled gently as he looked at Sarah who was still under his embrace of Josh. He walked back towards the room where they had seen the corpse of Cherishev, he looked around to see if he could find anything useful in the crime scene for his case. Andriy seemed to have done a clean job, and he had left no trace. David had no forensic support in Ukraine and retrieving the bullet might not prove useful as he couldn't work with it. His case had taken a blow when he allowed Kilitchsko go away but at the same time it had been blown wide open, he knew what he had to do and that was find the man that escaped, and he'd be a step closer to solving the case.

He was still there when he heard footsteps approaching the shed, he looked through the window and found men carrying AKM rifles approaching the building, Andriy must have informed his team. They had to get out of here but how? They might have surrounded the building, rushing out might prove costly but staying inside had the same outcome. They couldn't afford to stay inside if they wanted to stay alive. David rushed out of the office to inform Josh and Sarah who obviously had an idea that they had people on to them. Josh had a contraption in his hand, David walked close to him and whispered, "What's that?"

He responded, "It's a bomb, do you see this place, it's laced with materials needed to make all kinds of explosives." Josh walked to the entrance door of the shed, placing the bomb just over the door enough that opening the door would trigger the explosion, the trio stayed at the back exit, with no weapon, they stood with farm tools that they had found idle waiting for the intruders to enter from whichever exit.

They had sealed off all doors, preventing entry, it was too sudden, but they already had obstacles they were facing after being in Ukraine a few hours or less. David stood holding the pickaxe he had picked up firmly, he could hear his heartbeat as everywhere became exceedingly quiet, sweat running down his face as he stood expecting the unexpected. The doorknob twirled as though someone attempted to force open the door, the back doorknob twirled as well. They had been cornered and were in for a treat, the twirling continued for a while until there was a bang on the front door, the hit on the door forced the door open triggering the explosion. For a contraption constructed in a hurry, the explosion rocked the building, a thunderous sound swept through the perimeter as every one of them went flying to the ground. David and his team had assumed brace positions for impact as it had not much impact on them, the intruders were on the floor not dead but had incurred significant damage. They dragged themselves up, the whistling sound sounding in David's ears as he tried to find his balance. He held on to a beam that held the roof of the house in place. In a few seconds, he was back to normal and that meant one thing, any of the intruders that hadn't been killed would be back to normal.

They had to exit the shed and find safety else they'd be dead in no time, true to his predictions, the intruders at the back door opened fire on the shed. The sounds of gunfire filled the air as David took cover, lying gown on the floor with his hands on his head. Josh and Sarah laid down on the floor, trying to find an opening to escape. Josh still had a contraption in his hand, waiting for the right time to use it. The shooting lasted a few seconds and calm returned to the shed, the walls filled with holes, one could see what was going on inside the building from outside. The doorknob twirled yet again and this time, it opened, a boot entered the shed as they all remained quiet, Josh firmly held to his contraption of a bomb. Just when the door opened completely, he tossed it towards the door as the trio got up and made from the opening in the shed caused by the explosion.

As they fled the shed, another explosion rocked the shed, the vibrations, and waves vast, it pushed them a few meters away from the explosion to the floor, they could barely hear anything as David covered his ears with his hands. It looked to David like the danger had been averted but as they lay on the floor, they started to hear the sounds of oncoming vehicles and it wasn't just one or two, it was a lot, they dragged themselves up as they ran into the woods. From the words, they beheld pickup trucks filled with heavily armed militiamen. "It seems our friend Andriy had called for backup. Our task here in Ukraine just got a lot harder than it was supposed to. We have to find Andriy at all cost and then we can find out more about Igor Krishikov but for now, we have to get out of here before they start searching," David said to them

Josh and Sarah had no opposition to the idea of running away. They started walking deep into the woods to give them a head start should their pursuers decide to follow them.

CHAPTER TWENTY:

STRIKE AGAIN

In London, Roger and Andrew had been at the evidence locker trying to make sense of what they had obtained from the initial attack. Nothing was making any sense, it was a rather quiet day with not much happening their way, Roger sighed as he said to Andrew, "I'd have preferred it, had I gone with David to Ukraine, I'm sure they must have in a flashy way solved a case or avoided death or something but I'm stuck here looking through evidence, this isn't what I signed up for you know?" Andrew knew all too well the feeling of a young agent eager to impress and make for himself a name or better yet, serve to fill the enormous boots his father and grandfather had left for him. Andrew was once like him, eager to impress but over the years he had learnt that why there is the need to make a name for yourself, you mustn't always jump into action. Every action taken has a possibility of two outcomes, you could live to tell the tale or you might not be so lucky.

Andrew looked at Roger as he said to him, "Being an agent isn't always about making a name for yourself. It's about doing well and staying in the shadows. It's not about the fame, it's about the dedication. Know your heart is in the right place but try and do less with the attention, it might corrupt your focus." Roger kept quiet as Andrew talked, he knew in his heart that he loved Britain just as much as anybody in the service, but he loved being tagged a super spy a lot.

He responded, "Who says I can't love Britain and save her with grace? I can solve my cases in the flashiest way possible." He displayed a salsa dance move. "I was born to dazzle and I intend doing just that," he added.

Andrew laughed as he said, "Your desire for action might be your undoing, stay humble and you'll get to the top. Your father said something to me when I was a rookie agent working with him on a big case, he said that I should never go out there looking for action, that if I was looking in the right direction, the action would come to me. It didn't make sense to me, but I learnt eventually that once you are barking the right trees in cases, asking the right questions, looking at the right files, the action would come to you. It's a simple matter. That was your father's opinion, I hope it makes sense to you."

The pair spent time at the evidence locker of the MI6 trying to find clues when Andrew received a call, "This is Captain Dan James with the metropolitan police, am I speaking with a special agent Andrew Charlton?"

Andrew replied, "Affirmative Captain, what is the situation?"

"We have a situation agent, more like multiple situations and I've been told you were the one to call in situations such as these."

"You have the right number Captain, what is going on I repeat?"

The captain struggled to calm himself to relay his message in the best possible way, "We are under attack agent, we have multiple hostiles at Kensington Square, they have explosives strapped to themselves threatening to blow themselves up and the hostages if they aren't listened to, we responded to distress calls trying to sort out the problem but we just received yet another distress call, simultaneously, there is also an attack at Hyde Park. I haven't seen something like this before agent, we need your help, and we need the military if possible. There are multiple hostages, some shot dead, others injured. It's a mess agent. Get us all the help you can get."

Andrew stood up from the chair immediately after the captain finished talking, he asked with a stern voice, "Are all your coppers with you? Because you'll need all of them you can get and even more." Roger listened as Andrew traded words with the captain over the phone with an expression that gave the idea there was trouble, he started sorting out the documents they had been scavenging through hoping to file them properly before they left. Andrew finished the call and shouted at Roger, "We don't have all day Lad, London is on fire, we can't afford to file those, and we have to be out there." Roger left them on the table as the pair left the locker.

They headed straight for the garage where Andrew's Mercedes was parked, Roger had his Volkswagen Golf not far off. "We have multiple attacks going on simultaneously, we can't be at the same place, I am going to head for Kensington and you to Hyde Park if you can, we have to handle this. No panic childand most importantly, don't go looking for actions, let the actions come to you." They both drove off as fast as they could, Andrew to Kensington and Roger to Green and Hyde Park.

Kensington Park

Andrew drove as fast he could, he changed gears like he was in an episode of *Top Gear*, he had only one thing on his mind and it wasn't definite, he thought as he drove a plan to foil the attack. The last time ISIS struck, the plan was to leave no survivors, he hoped for all their sakes that that wasn't the plan they had this time. It was a long drive, he paid no attention to driving rules and passers-by, he drove like a man possessed, a man with a goal that would not be deterred no matter what stood by his side. He had captain Dan James on the phone, giving him feedback. He asked the captain, "What is the extent of damage that he could cause should his bomb go off?"

"I'm not sure agent, he's positioned at the entrance of Heythrop College, we can't say for sure his blast radius, but we are sure the casualties would be significant. We can't talk of him blowing up agent, we have to stop him before that happens."

Andrew was more confused now than he had been his entire career, he didn't know what he had to do, he had hostages and shooting him might trigger the explosion, but it was a choice he wasn't sure he wanted to take, he still had the captain on the other end of the phone as he asked him, "Have you established communications already Captain?"

"Negative sir, we just got to the scene and I opted to call you."

Andrew told him, "I'll be there in five minutes, hold on for me while I establish communications and find a way into the Heythrop College to destabilize whatever it is they got going on." The captain agreed to the plan but before he could drop the call, Andrew asked him yet again, "Do you have any update on the number of hostiles in there?"

"We have thermal sensors indicating that there's just three of them around the entrance of the college, we couldn't set them apart from some of the students in there, it's tough to ascertain the right information with the number of people in the building at the moment but I'll still try harder and let you know."

"Thanks captain, see you soon."

The certainty of the captain's formation was a spur for Andrew. The moment he dropped the call, he pressed his foot on the clutch, pulling the fear stick to the very extreme of its reaches, propelling the car forward as he hit top speed in a rush to arrive just in time to avoid any more casualties or injuries.

He got there in under five minutes, truncating his driving as he jumped off the car while it still moved, he rushed over to the captain who stood over his car with a phone to his ear, Andrew asked him, "What is the update Captain?"

"They have established communications, they have demanded someone of importance come in to take their orders personally or they detonate the explosives killing themselves and a significant number of students inside Heythrop College."

"Do we have any update on the explosives they are carrying? I have a plan, if we can have their focus on their demands, I can sneak into the college somehow to stop them from the inside. I need you to play along and get them someone to hear their demands since they can't tell you on the phone."

"What would you need to help you in your plan?"

"The plan was forged as I drove so I don't have all the parts in harmony so if you could help me with a way into the college, I'd be pleased." The captain smiled, he couldn't piece the plan together, but he could enquire from others. As they discussed, one of the coppers that stood beside the captain tapped the captain on the shoulders, it seemed he had a plan. He was a rookie and was young, but he seemed to know something that might benefit all of them. The private spoke to the captain in hushed tones that Andrew couldn't hear, Andrew growing restless raised his voice, "We don't have all day here son, if you have a plan, I reckon you go on and say it to all of us." The private looked at the agent who had worry written all over his face, he had a job to do and had no way of doing it.

The young private was unsure of how his information could be of help in saving the day, "I studied for a while in Heythrop, I know a thing or two about the campus, there is a tunnel designed underneath the school that we usually went through when I was there, it takes you all the way to the extreme end of the Kensington Square just behind the park towards Hyde Park, we'd always use it to sneak out while in school, if you can access it, you can find a way of getting into Heythrop." Andrew had his gaze fixed at the private, but his mind was somewhere else.

He looked at the captain next, "I know why they took the two parks that were extremely close to each other, they might be short-manned and they need to transport themselves through from Hyde to Kensington and the best possible way is through the tunnel that he just spoke of."

Andrew picked up his phone and put a call through to Roger at Hyde Park. If they were going to repel these attacks, they had to work together. Andrew removed his 9mm handgun from his trousers, checked the cartridge to see how many rounds he had, checked his jacket to confirm he had extra cartridges. He held the captain on his shoulders and assured him that he'd be back with good news, "Hold the fort captain, the best way to disrupt this is to go at it from inside, take me to the tunnel entrance private and try to be discreet. I don't know why but I think they'd be there trying to protect the entrance. Captain, I need you to do me a favour, if you hear gunshots from the entrance, I need you to send at least five men for support, I am not taking the men with me now because I don't want to spook them so they don't detonate the explosives yet, once I have them, you and your men can swoop in and make the clearance. Do you understand me, Captain?"

"Loud and clear."

Hyde Park

Roger arrived at Hyde Park where he met a shopping mall amount of coppers stationed outside in front of the Grand Hotel. He stopped his car, ran to the officer in charge and said as he struggled to find his breath, "I am Special Agent Roger Moore, what's the situation?"

The officer in charge, Captain James Target, responded, "Agent, we got distress calls of multiple hostiles in the Grand Hotel, so we mobilized. Since we arrived, we have been trying to communicate with them, but we've not gotten a response. I can't help but feel like they are refusing to communicate. There is also an attack happening now at Kensington Park. I don't know what is going on but these attacks are becoming too much."

Roger answered him, "I am well aware of the attack at Kensington, I have a partner over there right now, let's leave that aside and focus on what's going on here, I trust they can handle situations over there. Do you know how many of them we have in here?"

The captain replied, "We have thermal images of just three armed men in the building but if we can't hear from them, we can't force our way into the hotel. We don't want to trigger a series of events that might end up in the death of the hostages, seeing as they are our number one priority."

"Is there any way I can enter into the Grand Hotel save the main entrance?"

"There is but they've got it covered. Thermal images report one of the armed intruders as stationed at the rear door behind the Grand Hotel."

Roger was worried as his phone rang, he looked at it and it was Andrew. He was excited to hear from Andrew, he picked the phone up and asked him, "What's the situation over there?"

Andrew cut in and Roger could feel the tension in his voice, Andrew asked him, "What's the nature of the attack at Hyde Park?"

"They've taken Grand Hotel and a few hostages, I'm at the scene now trying to sort it all out."

Andrew replied, "I don't think they've got Grand Hotel, or anywhere in Hyde Park for that matter, I need you to go in, their target is Kensington but I just found out there was a tunnel link between Hyde Park and Kensington. I needed to be sure where they had attacked in Hyde Park and when you said Grand Hotel, I knew it was just a distraction, the tunnel is just behind the Grande Hotel. I could be wrong but I need you to go into the Grande Hotel, alone if I might add and try to meet me out back so we can access the tunnel together. They've used the tunnel as a link to Kensington. I wondered why but I just found out now even though the police were trying to keep it low key that the foreign secretary is giving a speech at the Heythrop, he is their target, the Grande Hotel was a distraction. I need you ASAP."

It didn't make much sense to Roger, he asked wanting to clear his doubts, "They have taken Kensington already, why would they still need Hyde Park, it would amount to dividing their powers and weakening their hold on Kensington, I don't understand what you mean."

Andrew knew it would be hard to understand and accept but he had a gut feeling that he was right, he was already at the tunnel entrance as he said, "I know they have Kensington already, but it's not a move to weaken their strength Lad, it's a move to weaken ours. If we are focused on Hyde Park and Kensington, we won't be able to put full efforts on one and it would give them the chance to make away with the foreign secretary. I have a bigger fear and I hope I am wrong, but it looks most likely."

Roger was worried at this point, he asked, "What is this fear in your mind? It shouldn't be as horrible as you are making it sound."

"It is that horrible. I have a gut feeling that they aren't here for the rest of the hostages, thermal imagery suggests they are just three insurgents in the Heythrop building but I doubt the authenticity of that, I think they might be more, I think they have just one exit plan and that is using the foreign secretary as bait, I'm not certain but I think that's the plan, it's a divide and conquer strategy. Make your way into the Grande

Hotel, find their man and meet me out back, free the hostages."

CHAPTER TWENTY-ONE: RESCUE

Roger dropped his call, picked his handgun tucked in his trouser, he checked his trigger to decide if he had rounds, he checked his gun carrier for rounds, he had enough to go in, he rested on the side of his car, made his way to the entrance door of the Grande Hotel, a glass door that allowed whoever was inside to see what was going on. He peeked through the door where he saw just one intruder with a rifle in his hand, he couldn't barge in as that would mean danger for the hostages and himself, he sneaked to the side of the building, there was an open window, all that mattered was making sure he wasn't seen. He wondered if he could avoid entering the Grande Hotel and head for the tunnel that Andrew spoke of as he knew their target was the Heythrop but he knew that would leave the hostages in the Grande Hotel in more risk, he had to go in one way or the other, take the three armed men down and then head for Kensington.

He made his way for the window, hoping the intruders wouldn't be around the window and they wouldn't find him, luckily for him, the window entrance led to a storage compartment deep in the storage section of the Grande Hotel. He opened the window as quiet as he could and sneaked in. Coming down, he missed his step as he fell into a cluster of cleaning buckets and mops, his fall made a sound that attracted the intruders, he was up to his feet in no time but had sustained a cut on his left arm that was bleeding. He picked up a shopping mall cloth from a closet and applied pressure to his cut as he tried to escape the storage compartment. On his way out, he heard sounds as he took cover in a shopping maller broom storage, it was really cramped, the smell of unwashed fabric played around his senses, it was difficult for him to tolerate but he had no choice, it was that or be seen by the intruder. He consoled himself with the fact that there were just three of them.

He stayed quiet the whole time trying not to move an inch or make a single sound. One of the terrorists came into the room and saw the buckets scattered all over the floor. He walked towards the buckets worried that someone had entered the hotel. He saw the blood, looked up and saw the window open, he was about to get back to his feet when Roger jumped him, with a thick rope, he suffocated the terrorist. His grip firm on both sides of the rope as he pulled it against his neck, the intruder struggled, but Roger found a way to distance himself from the intruder, the grip was tight but the intruder struggled to stay conscious. Roger placed his right foot on the back of the terrorist as he pressed his body forward pulling his neck backwards with the rope. He struggled over and over until he started to lose breath, he stopped trying to hold Roger and made attempts to free his neck from the rope, but Roger held firm, he made desperate attempts but life had already started to leave him, after a few seconds, he was out. Roger let him down gently, not wanting him to make a sound.

With one down, Roger just had two left, he sneaked past the door of the storage compartment, checked his wristwatch, he had been inside the Grande Hotel for a few minutes, he couldn't tell if Andrew was still outside waiting for him but he had to hurry if he was going to make it in time to support Andrew infiltrate Kensington. He hid behind a door that led to the lobby as he looked into the lobby and saw two armed men walking around the place with a lot of hostages sitting down on the floor, he needed a plan to divide them so he could take them on one after the other, he stood there a few seconds, looking into the lobby, his eyes met the gaze of a child who was lying down like every other hostage, the childlooked at him, he smiled as did the child. The intruders looked at the child as they heard him laughing. Just about the time they noticed, Roger threw a shopping mall plastic far away from him which made a sound that was loud considering the quietness at the hotel lobby at the time.

He heard voices as one of the terrorist ordered the other to check it out, "Ya Olek, you heard that too right, go check it out." The other terrorist murmured as he headed towards the hallway just behind the lobby, he walked into the hallway, facing the direction where the sound came from which was directly opposite Roger's hiding spot, when he passed, Roger closed the door slowly behind him to make it look like he had closed it. He saw the plastic bottle on the floor, bent down to pick it up. He got up and turned around to report the cause of the sound but right there in front of him, Roger had his 9mm handgun pointing in his face.

Roger spoke gently to him, "I'd stay quiet if I were you, if you as much as make a sound, I'll shoot you in the face," Roger held his handgun firmly, one wrong move and a hostage could die or better yet, he could die. He wasn't going to shoot either because if he did, it could alert the other who could contact his partners at Kensington. Olek didn't know that, but Roger was in a tighter position than he was and he was the one with a gun in his face.

Olek had a sick smile on his face as he said to Roger in a really accented voice, "You can't shoot me, you shoot me and my partner opens fire in all the hostages, my life is not very important, but I don't think it's the same for them, you can't afford to have them killed."

Roger had been pushed back to the corner he was trying to avoid, Olek knew what he could and couldn't do so he tried to bluff, "I don't mind one bit, if you as much as take a single step, I am going to send you to your maker quicker than you think." Olek started walking towards him non-stop, he took steps backwards, hoping Olek would consider the 9mm in his face. The big Ukrainian walked closer, for every step he took, Roger went backwards, he was closer than usual and just as Roger was about to take another step, he hit the wall, he was at the end of the lobby.

Olek charged towards him fiercely, throwing a ferocious fist his way but Roger ducked with Olek's powerful fist hitting the wall behind him but it had no real effect on the terrorist as he removed his hand like nothing had happened, he threw yet another powerful punch this time, a shopping mall portion of his fist making contact with the face of Roger as he tried to avoid it, it caught his left cheek as he tried to avoid it, the punch was fierce as Roger lost his balance, pain shot through his face but he had to tolerate not to make a sound to attract the other man. He was cornered and Olek knew he had him where he wanted him. With a sinister smile on his face, Olek cracked his knuckle joints and his neck as he walked towards Roger, with every step he made himself bigger giving Roger the impression that there was nothing he could do to get out of this situation.

Roger trembled as he was approached, he still had his 9mm pointed at Olek, but it served no true purpose at the moment, it was nothing to Olek because he couldn't use it. Roger tucked it so he could use his fist properly, he tucked his gun in his pistol carrier that he had on his chest. Raised his fists over his face gesturing his intentions to trade punches with Olek but he had to be careful not to make a sound and also not to get killed. He tried to avoid being too close to Olek so he started to take steps back but he was already at the edge of the building so he started to turn around while he faced Olek. He knew his skills in hand-to-hand combat, what he had problems with was the fact that Olek was obviously stronger than him, Olek knew he had him cornered and was eager to finish him off.

The big Ukrainian charged at him and started throwing multiple punches at him, Roger maintained his calm just avoiding them as best he could, he could feel the force of each punch when it passed his face, he knew getting hit by two or three of those would be really damaging to his chances of success, he avoided them for a while tiring Olek out a little and at that point, he realized he could strike back as he had evened the playing field. He brought his fist forward like he meant business, Olek threw yet another punch and he dodged yet again, he knew he might have reduced efficiency if he hit Olek with his fist so he threw an elbow at the big man, making contact with his lower jaw, it was a fierce hit as Olek lost a tooth,

Roger knew he had the upper hand now, he charged landing multiple blows on different points in Olek's body, the chest, the abdomen and sometimes the face. Olek was cornered on the wall, he knew he was losing ground on the fight and wanted to scream but Roger wouldn't let him, Roger continued to land punches on his jaw allowing him to shriek in pain, it was punch after punch as Olek was slowly losing his feet, falling to the ground, Roger had no intention of stopping, he had stopped using both of his fist, he used just one as he held Olek's head from behind with the other, he kept hitting him over and over and over until Olek could barely move, the Ukrainian terrorist was on the floor unable to respond. He wasn't taking any chance, he went for the storage unit and found a rope, bound Olek's hands and legs as he left him there.

He was still binding Olek when he heard the other man shout out, "Olek, where are you, I told you to check out a single sound and still you refuse to come back." The voice was getting closer, Roger stood behind the door. The constant call but no reply for Olek made him worry. The terrorist took out his rifle, pointing it in front of him. This one wasn't as big as Olek. Andrew had be waiting for Roger already and he had spent over thirty minutes at the Grande Hotel, he had his pocketknife in his hand, waiting patiently. He saw the nozzle of the rifle enter the door and he silenced his breathing. The nozzle entered and the rest of the gun followed. Once Roger saw the face, he attacked him with the knife stabbing him multiple times with the knife on his neck, the terrorist dropped the gun as he made attempts to stop the stabbing but he could do nothing against it, constantly, stab after stab, Roger pummelled his knife in and out of his neck as blood splattered all over the walls. He made sure by the time he was done, the terrorist was on the floor, dead, his hand over the stab wounds and his eyes open. Roger could care less how gruesome his death was as he made his way towards the hostages that sat down in the lobby afraid for their lives.

Roger ran into the lobby blood stains all over his body, the hostages seeing him started screaming but he calmed them down, "I am Roger Moore, I'm one of the good guys, don't you worry, the situation is under control, I need you all to head on out of the hotel, there are coppers out there that will attend to your every need." The hostages, happy they were safe, hurriedly made for the exit as Roger headed for the rear exit of the Grande Hotel, he opened the door, his gun in his hand and blood on his shirt. He looked and saw Andrew standing with the rookie a couple hundred meters away, he ran over to Andrew. He got there panting, his breath was exceedingly heavy as he needed to settle down so he could speak.

Andrew waited for Roger to calm down before he asked anything, Roger noticed the look on his face, "What, haven't you ever seen blood before?"

Andrew laughed a little as he responded, "I'm guessing you took my advice about waiting for action, but it seems the action came at you a little angry. What is up with you all covered in blood and what took you so long?"

Roger looked at him, "For starters, you could have told me I could avoid the Grande Hotel situation and meet you out here, why would you do that? The least you could do is come help me out."

"I apologize, you wouldn't have wanted my help, you have a thing for making the most out of every situation, I thought you doing it by yourself would do good for your ego plus someone had to save the hostages in there and it had to be you, someone who knows or at least have an idea of the agenda of the attacks by ISIS. Now, let's move on from what I did or didn't do and focus on what we have to do to fix the current situation."

Roger sighed as he got closer to the tunnel, he looked at the young man standing beside Andrew, "Who's he? Judging from the uniform, he's a copper but why is he the only one here?"

"He was the one who told me about this entrance so he brought me here." He looked at the rookie cop and told him, "I'm going to need a favour from you, run back to the captain and tell him to split his manpower, some stationed in front of Heythrop and a few other stationed out here and they should be armed and ready because the people they might see coming out from this tunnel will be armed and dangerous. Go lad." The rookie ran as fast as his feet could carry him, looking back occasionally as he headed for the captain.

Andrew looked at Roger as they both shared a smile, Andrew with a smirk on his face said to Roger, "Let's go save ourselves a foreign secretary."

CHAPTER TWENTY-TWO:
FOREIGN SECRETARY

The pair entered the tunnel as carefully as they could, Andrew first and then Roger afterwards. Inside the tunnel was moist, it smelled like damped clothes, they could hear rats running and water rested on the tunnel floor. Just up ahead there was light, it illuminated just the edge of the tunnel that led to a shopping mall door, the light made them realize that whatever door linked the Heythrop to the tunnel was open. Andrew brought out his 9mm, they held on to their guns firmly hoping they'd not have to use them. Shooting would inform the terrorists of their presence and would put the hostages at risk.

They got close to the exit and they started to hear voices, two voices precisely speaking a language that sounded like Russian. Those guys left there to be the lookout. Roger and Andrew got close to the exit that was upwards, attached to the wall was a short fence not much taller than Roger. They stayed still, paying attention to the men. One of the men walked away, Roger sighed, *Just in time*. Roger looked at Andrew, with one of his fingers pointed upwards, he held on to the ladder trying to climb into the open exit. Andrew picked up the hint of the plan as he made a sound that attracted the standing man to the hole, he got close and put his head just in time for Roger to grab him by the back and pulled him into the hole. He made a thud on the ground of the tunnel not making enough noise to attract others.

He fell on the floor losing grip of his gun, Andrew stood in the dark where he couldn't see, he got up trying to pick up his gun, but Andrew held him with one of his hands on his jaws and the other on his head, he grunted trying to free himself but not in time as Andrew snapped his neck, he fell on the floor lifeless. Roger escaped the hole and went for the door that exited a room, it looked dusty like an ancient study. He hid behind the door as the other man that left the room was approaching. Andrew who had no idea had his just outside the hole when the man saw him, he rushed towards him to attack Andrew but Roger jumped him in time, hitting him with the cartridge of his gun as he fell motionless to the floor. Roger helped Andrew up, they tied him up, stuffing his mouth with clothing, tying him up so he couldn't shout. The pair headed for the auditorium where they had the hostages in Heythrop College. Andrew looked carefully from where they hid themselves if he could find the foreign secretary, but he didn't, he saw three armed men standing around the hostages.

Andrew signalled to Roger, who looked at him immediately, he whispered as low as he could, "The foreign secretary isn't there, I'm going to go look for him elsewhere." Crouching, he crawled away from the auditorium trying to locate where the foreign minister could be, Roger stayed out trying to find a way to free the hostages, Andrew wondered as he crawled away where they could have kept the secretary, thermal imagery had presented just three armed men and they were all there, who else could be in here. He was crawling when his phone rang, not thinking anyone could call him at the time, coupled with the silence in the auditorium, the phone ringing was as loud as can be, the sound sweeping through the open hallways.

The intruders, angry at the prospect of someone still holding a phone and probably not in the mix of hostages, started shouting at the top of their voice. One more agitated than the others, brought out his rifle, cocked his AKM rifle as he shouted, "If you know it was your phone, you better stand up else I'll start killing people one after the other." He had no accent in his voice, and he was British. The hostages began to panic. Roger could hear them cry as he looked at Andrew who had stood up trying to make his way to a safe spot to hide. The phone kept ringing as Andrew finally brought it out, it was an unknown number, he hid himself behind a door as he took the call, "Who is this? This is definitely not a good time."

It was the rookie cop, and he had information for Andrew. He could tell from Andrew's muffling response that he had made a mistake. He replied stuttering, "I am so sorry sir, I just wanted you to know that there are more than three, thermal imagery just reported six more armed men and one unarmed man kneeling down in the top floor of the building, towards the west end." He said hurriedly as he dropped the call.

Andrew didn't know whether to thank him or not, his information was timely as it'd saved Andrew the stress of searching the entire building for the secretary, but the call might have jeopardized their entire mission. Meanwhile, the terrorists were threatening the hostages to give up whoever it was that had the phone that rang. He readied his rifle wanting to start shooting when Roger walked out of hiding, he hid his gun. With his hands raised, he walked out with his shirt covered in blood. One of the intruders walked up to him, looked at him keenly as he hit his mouth with his gun, Roger fell to the floor, holding his jaw.

Another approached Roger with his rifle pointing to him, he shouted, "Whose blood

is that? Answer me, who did you kill?"
Roger shook his head indicating he had
killed no one but they wouldn't agree. They
threw a punch at him which connected with
his nostril, he screamed in pain as the
hostages all quelled in fear. The terrorists
landed blow after blow all over Roger as he
covered his face with the attacks landing all
over his back, abdomen and ribs. One
shouted at the others, you go check on
Boyka and Ivanovic, if they are not there,
come back immediately, we'll put him
down." Roger looked at him, he had
explosives strapped to his body, but it
seemed to him like the bomb was
deactivated at the time. He wished in his
heart that he had Josh's knowledge. There
was a digital screen on his abdomen, but it
had nothing displaying on it.

He laid still as the other two left the room.
Not moving, the terrorist attempted to kick
him in his abdomen but he pushed back his
body reducing contact but creating enough

space for his hand to grab the legs as he held firm, pulling him to the ground. Roger threw punches at the intruder randomly hitting him all over his face, blood spilled from his nose as Roger was relentless in landing the punches, he wouldn't stop for no reason, even after the terrorist was unconscious, he still didn't stop, he landed punch after punch until he was sure he wouldn't stand up. He turned behind him when he heard a footstep, he wasn't sure it was the right move but he picked up the intruders rifle, facing the door, he wasn't ready to die, if whoever walks in through that door made the wrong decision, he would send him to thy kingdom come, he'd have a minutes window to wait the hostages if he did that, he wasn't sure if that was the right decision but if he didn't make that move, he'd die himself.

The door creaked open slowly, he gently rubbed his index finger against the trigger waiting to end it for whoever came in, to his surprise and pleasure, Andrew opened the door with blood stains on his body as well. Roger was exceedingly happy to see the man, he said to him with joy on his face, "You didn't go look for the secretary?"

Andrew stammered as he told him, "It was my phone that rang, if I had left you alone, you'd be dead by now and I couldn't do that, your life is worth just as much to me."

Roger said with a smirk on his face, "I had it all under control. If you doubt me, you can ask these good people, I gave them something to thrill them."

"Don't get so cocky boy, let's go for the foreign secretary, our mission here is almost over but it can't be until we find what we are looking for."

Roger looked at the hostages, who had relief written over their faces, "What about them?"

"We need them to stay put, should they go outside and are seen by the rest of them, it'd put the foreign secretary's life in danger." He looked at the hostages who were desperately in need of an order to follow and said, "I need you all to do me a favour, you are safe but I need you to remain here a while, when it's the right time for you to go out, I will come and give you that information myself but for now please I beg you, just stay put."

The people murmured among themselves a while but were ready to heed the words of Andrew. The pair left them picking two rifles as main weapons and keeping their handguns as a side arm. They sneaked down the lobby heading straight for the stairs that led to the top floor, the only floor above the ground floor. Up the stairs, the hid on the wall, looking down the hallway towards the left wing of the building, they saw two men standing outside, keeping guard over a room door. Andrew looked at Roger who was behind him and couldn't see anything, "We have two hostiles in front of the room we are trying to access, we have to get them out somehow." Roger thought of a plan as he screamed loud enough for the intruders to hear and they came running over, Roger and Andrew ran down the stairs as quietly as they could still making the same sound.

One of them stood over at the stairs looking down to see what or who was making the sound, he signalled the other to head back that he'd check it himself and the other did as he was instructed, but as he walked away, he could hear muffled sounds like someone struggling to speak but his mouth was covered, he rushed in, heading down the stairs when Andrew hit him with a rifle knocking him out. Andrew picked up his phone and called the rookie cop, "What's the status on the thermal imagery?"

He replied, "We have four armed in the room I mentioned earlier and two approaching the door with rifles." Andrew commended his efforts.

Andrew and Roger were at the door of the supposed room, they could hear dialogue in the room, but they weren't sure how to go about it. Things were falling in place when they heard one telling the others to gather the rest of the terrorists save one at the lobby and another at the exit. The footsteps that approached the door were two so Andrew and Roger took cover in the office just opposite the one they were coming from, they passed and went their way. When they were out of sight, Roger knocked on the door and the voice, in anger, screamed in Russian as it headed for the door, immediately the door was opened, Andrew jumped in smacking his nose with the gun, Roger shot straight at the other standing close to the window, three times in the chest and he fell down on his chest as blood flowed slowly out his lifeless body.

The gun shot alerted the others, who had been sent to get the rest of the team and also the metropolitan police officers that stood outside. Andrew signalled to Roger to the foreign secretary under the table that stood in the office and Roger did as he was told. They assumed perfect hiding positions waiting for the intruders to return and just as they planned. The two men opened the door shouting the names of their comrades but found them on the floor dead, as they turned round in an attempt to run away, they heard the sounds of cockpit guns behind them. Two British intelligence officers had guns pointed at their heads. One made an attempt to reach for his gun but Roger gave him a disclaimer, "I wouldn't do that if I were you, there's no way you'd reach your gun before I'd pull the trigger." The terrorist thought being killed was better than being arrested, he still made an attempt for his gun but Roger shot him straight in the head, straight to the ground.

The sound his lifeless body made as it touched the ground was an eye opener for the second one, who immediately raised his hand in the air. He knew that neither Roger nor Andrew had time to waste and any wrong move by him would mean his definite death. Andrew brought out his phone and contacted the captain, "Captain, this is agent Andrew Charlton, I call to inform you that the hostages are free and the attackers out of commission, you can send your men into the Heythrop to take the hostages out." The captain remained speechless.

The foreign secretary came out from his place of hiding when he felt that all was under control, he had an expression of joy in his face as he said to Andrew and Roger, "Thank you lads, you have done a great good for Britain and for me, your nation thanks you and I thank you. Say the word and I'll make it happen. Whatever reward it is that you want, just let me know."

Andrew replied, "This wasn't about reward. It's what we do." They led the intruder out of the building by hand as Roger remembered the other one that they had bound down by the tunnel entrance into the building. He let Andrew take the man away as he went downstairs to get the other whom he found still lying down struggling to free himself, he picked him up as he headed outside of the Heythrop.

The hostages had already been released as they went out to loved ones and friends. Andrew and Roger walked out of Heythrop with the foreign secretary in between both of them and the two terrorists they had captured on either side, they handed the men to the captain requesting they be kept separately for interrogation by no one else but themselves. The foreign secretary was unhurt but they both looked like a mess, covered in blood. The captain approached them but unlike every other person out there, his expression wasn't as happy. Andrew asked, "What is the matter with you? Two possible mass murders have been averted and you look this sad? Is there any other problem?"

The captain reluctantly mentioned, "There was another attack on a shopping maller scale at the Women's Health Clinic Dulwich."

The agents looked at themselves, wondering the cause for the attacks all in one day as Roger said to the men, "We'll go check it out." The pair got to Andrew's car as Roger took the wheels, still covered in blood, the pair made their way for the women's health clinic.

CHAPTER TWENTY-THREE: A STUMBLING BLOCK

Roger drove through the streets of London like he was in a Dakar Rally, he said to Andrew as he hit speeds that neither men thought possible in London, "Fasten your seatbelt old man and hold on to dear life, this drive isn't getting any smoother." Andrew laughed as he held tight with his seatbelt already fastened. In less to no time, they were at the clinic. The car parked in front, they rushed in, the casualties and injuries lined up not too much, coppers and medics trying to attend to the wounded and others rounding up the dead.

They went in to count the dead who had been readied for the morgue with their names on it. Roger looked at all of them. He looked at Andrew before he made the move as he said to him, "We were focused trying to save Kensington and Hyde Park not knowing something like this was going on here, what kind of agents are we if we can't save everyone?"

Andrew walked towards him, patted him on the shoulder as he replied to his question, "Saving everyone is something no one can do, we did the best we can do and averted a lot more deaths, I know it might not seem like much right now because of the ones you are looking at but I tell you lad, had we not stopped the deaths at Kensington Square, we could have registered a significant increase in the number of deaths. I don't want you to think of today as a failure, I want you to see it as a steppingstone to ending this menace. We already have two in our custody and when we get back, we'll get all the information we can about them. Hopefully David, Sarah and Josh will come back with something, I believe we will fix all this and then you won't feel so down cast by the death that happened here. Chin up lad, you did very well today and I'm extremely proud of you."

As they spoke, a doctor approached them with information on the dead, he called

Andrew asking him, "Are you the officer in charge?" Andrew nodded his head in response as the doctor continued speaking, "There is something that you must know, there are five dead, each with multiple gunshot wounds on the thoracic region but there's one, a Carla Scarlet, a heavily pregnant woman who has no gunshot wound, I presume she died of shock but without an autopsy done, we can't be sure." Andrew stopped talking, he froze wanting words to respond with as did Roger.

Andrew managed to find the right words to ask series of questions, "Did you say Carla Scarlet? Wife to one David Scarlet?" The doctor checked his charts and nodded his head. Andrew asked again, "You are sure she has no gunshot wounds? You suspect she died of shock?"

The doctor replied, "I am of the opinion, you see it was really fierce here a while ago. We weren't sure any of us would make it, the fear got even worse when after a long while of being taken hostage, the police weren't coming for us, we thought in our hearts that we were done for, that no one would save us. True to our fears, no one came for us, for whatever reason known to them, the intruders just got up and left and she was heavily pregnant having multiple complications over and over again, it makes absolute sense that the shock could have killed her. I've tried to reach her husband, but I haven't been able to, I've tried to reach her parents who are usually always here but I haven't been able to get them, that's surprising because they were here this morning just before the attack and I never saw them leave, well I wouldn't know because I was trembling in fear but why would they leave their daughter behind?"

Andrew responded to the doctor, "I know her husband, we work together but you are not going to be able to get him right about now, I'll go over to her parents and break the news myself. Thanks, doctor, for your efforts, it's very well received." The doctor walked away as Andrew and Roger went through the corpses that laid on the bed with cloth covering them completely. Roger didn't know Carla, but Andrew had seen her a couple of times, he saw her corpse and covered his mouth with his hands as he told Roger, "We have to let Andrew know about this, she and her parents are the only family he has alongside a little girl he adopted recently. He is not going to take this very well but we have to tell him."

Roger had a different idea, "Telling him might take him out of the motion, you just said it yourself that she is the only family he has got, he'd be too heartbroken to continue with the mission, I think we should keep it to ourselves for a while, up until we solve this case, I know it just started but it looks to me like we already have a lead on the case with the terrorists we have arrested."

Andrew understood Roger's logic but it was David, he told Roger, "You are new to this world, they might call you the super spy but David is a man like no other, his devotion to his country is second to none, he had left his wife once while heavily pregnant to save his country and boy did he save Britain, he came back a hero to his wife and now again, he left her once again to save his country. Every other man would be too heartbroken to continue but that doesn't apply to David. He knows what he is doing, besides, I couldn't keep information like this away from someone I call a friend.

"He would be sad, losing a wife and an unborn childin the same day but like you heard from the doctor, it was shock that killed her, he can peg shock on anyone and would move on, not without pain but he'd move on none the less." Roger looked down not wanting to show his expression or say what was on his mind, but Andrew could tell, "You don't think she died of shock, do you?"

"I don't, it's too coincidental for comfort, and she has been in this same hospital a while now taking treatment but dies on the same day ISIS attacked. I can't help but feel like they found out that David was the officer in charge of project Declon after all, these people found a way to infiltrate a top-secret government bio-lab, this particular information would be a piece of cake for them to retrieve. This is a statement to David, to the rest of us and to the British government that they have a hold on us, that they have a hold on Britain and could do with us whatever they please."

Andrew placed his fingers on his jaws as he thought for a second, he said to Roger, "You might be right, you might not but let's stick with the doctor's professional opinion, check on her parents and then put a call through to David and tell him about this. It's been a long day, it was dark outside but the calm that's brought by the night usually had stayed away." London stayed awake mourning all that it had lost. Sirens of metropolitan police and ambulances filled the airs as no one found the needed peace to shut their eyes for the night. Andrew and Roger couldn't turn in for the night at least not yet, they needed some information about Carla's parents. David had lost a lot in one day, the least they could do was ensure that it wasn't all gone.

They informed the ambulance taking the bodies away that Carla should be taken to the London General Morgue that they'd handle the proceedings. Roger said to Andrew, "Let's make sure David still has but a single family." They drove away in Andrew's car as they headed to Carla's birth home.

"Multiple attacks in one day, kidnapping the foreign secretary, I understand, Hyde Park as a distraction, makes perfect sense but the women's health clinic, I don't get it. David's going to be really devastated when he finds out about Carla's passing. I just hope it doesn't take him out of action too much." Andrew said as they drove towards David's in-laws.

Roger asked, "Do you think David really would be okay with his wife passing?"

Andrew sighed, his hand on his head, "I can't say for sure, I've known David a while and I trust his resolve is great but this is his wife, a man almost never comes back from a loss of this magnitude but I really hope he does, ending this ISIS madness depends on his mental stability. He has really grown in the service, and I can't see a better leader for this team than David. I really hope he gets over this."

Roger wasn't done with the question, he asked yet again, "Back there at Kensington, you were so calm, I call myself a super spy but all the time, I thought about the possibility of failure, I wondered what would happen to the people if I made a mistake, even when your phone rang, you still handled the situation with so much calm and control. How do you do it?"

"I have my worries as well lad, I panicked too but I didn't let it get the better of me, success depends on completely trusting yourself and your teammates and despite your antics, I trust in your willingness and ability to protect the good people of Britain. It's not something you can't do having that level of confidence, you can, maybe even better than I can but you have to allow the action come to you and not vice versa. If you wait for the action to come to you, you'd have enough time to think of a perfect plan."

"I hope David has the same conviction as you do, I hope he can stay calm in the face of this distraction and finish this mission and save Britain first," Roger added.

Andrew replied, "I know he will, I trust him that much." The drive was fast, but the destination was far. Roger drove as fast as he could in a bid to save whatever they could of David's family.

They arrived at Carla's parents late at night, the entire environment calm under the control of night. Stopping in front of the building, they could see lights on inside and they could hear the television sounds, but they needed to go in to be sure that they were home and also inform them of Carla's demise. Andrew came down first as Roger parked the vehicle out front. The time was odd for the television to be on, Andrew brought out his gun as he held it firmly by his side, and Roger joined him as he gestured for Roger to go back so they could enter from both ends.

Roger readied his handgun as did Andrew on the main entrance, Andrew knocked gently waiting for a response but none came forth, he tried opening the door, but it was open. They entered the building, the place littered looking like the occupants had left in a hurry. Clothes on the floor, littered everywhere, the kitchen was intact, it looked to them like a robbery at the time, but Andrew noticed that Laura's jewellery was still intact in a shopping mall box just besides her dresser. She had a lot of valuable pieces, but none was gone. Andrew felt like something was off as he continued to pry, he made his way down the basement and found nothing suspicious. It occurred to them that the only things that had left the building were clothes and papers as a flat file containing documents laid on the floor in the master bedroom. "Something doesn't feel right, Roger."

Roger, looking at the place, responded, "It's either they were kidnapped or they left but why would they leave? I can say for sure it wasn't a robbery because if it were, the jewelleries wouldn't be here still, it wasn't murder as the scene don't suggest that, the doors don't look like it was forced open, it was opened willingly. Something's not right but I believe we have to find them first before we can come to any conclusion."

Andrew walked to the master room door, "Check out back, ensure that there's nothing out there, we have to rule out the possibility of murder and focus on finding them." Roger went out back, going through the entire yard just to be sure that they weren't missing anything. Andrew stood inside when his phone rang, it was an unknown foreign number.

It was David who quickly started speaking, "Andy, how's it going over there, we had an issue here but we are good, we are at a safe place for now. Cherishev that we came looking for is dead, we were attacked by a group, not sure if they were part of ISIS but they clearly didn't want us digging further into their operations. I called because I'm looking at the TV now and it's on the news that there were multiple terrorist attacks in London, what's the update?"

Andrew kept quiet for a short while before he continued, "David, you need to get back to London as quickly as you can, the attacks were coordinated, three of them, I don't know what's going on in Ukraine, but I can tell you for sure that the seat of ISIS's power has to be in London at the moment. Roger and I faced the biggest test of our careers yet but it's nothing compared to what awaits us, they have a master plan and they are playing by it."

"What about Roger? I hope he wasn't too overwhelmed with happenings?"

Andrew answered, "There are positives from today's attacks, and they are negatives as well but I need you to do me a favour, get on the next flight to London, you can leave Sarah and Josh over there to continue investigating if you must, but you have to come home."

"You are sounding different, what's going on?"

"We caught two of them at Kensington today where they had the foreign secretary hostage, we freed him as well, but we learnt something crucial, in their ranks aren't just Ukrainians and Russians and Kazakhs, they have English kids as well. I don't know what prompted English lads to want to attack their own home, but I killed some today. I killed English kids as I attempted to free the hostages and I didn't feel good about it. It was horrible. I tried to maintain my calm just so I don't spook Roger, but I don't know if he noticed they were English lads like himself trying to pull down their own country."

David tried to calm Andrew down, "It's the perks of the job, don't think of them as English lads, think of them as terrorists that have decided to team up with the enemies. I know it's never easy gunning down lads you presumed to be the leaders of tomorrow but plucking these bad elements actually gives us the chance to forge tomorrow with lads like Roger that love their country. You did pretty well saving the foreign secretary just the two of you, I will try to make it to London as quickly as I can but tomorrow isn't going to be possible. We were attacked by heavily armed men but thanks to Josh's ingenuity, we made it out alive and thanks also to Sarah's quick thinking, we could tail them back to their hideout. We might not be able to mount a serious challenge considering their numbers, but we will do what we can to get whatever information we can and we'll see what happens next after that. I have to say since we arrived in Ukraine, it has been one thing after another. I have one fear though."

Andrew listened keenly as David spoke, what could be his fear he wondered. "What is it that makes you worried?"

David reluctantly answered him, "We might be able to stop the usage of the Declon 5, we might be able to retrieve its files, but I doubt that we'd be able to stop ISIS, we might only be able to win each battle as they come but ending the war seems a task that's going to be almost impossible for us."

"Why do you think that?"

David continued, "I watched the news about how they made London stand still, I saw with my own eyes the damage done at Larimer, I saw yet again at Ukraine the determination they had to clean all evidences of their actions. I see in them the determination to fight a cause and knowing fully well why they are fighting. I can't tell you that they'd stop because I wouldn't and adding to the fact that they are already converting English kids and the fact that I think they have access to information. I doubt they'd go away easily. We can find Krishikov and kill him or lock him up, but they'd just get a new leader and continue. This is a fight that will continue beyond you or me, but I hope we can do our part to stop it in our time. I thank you once again for your efforts today but more of that will be needed for the fight that awaits us."

David was correct, he had seen their coordination today. For a handful of fighters, they had the entirety of London in their grasp and were able to force the British government into mobilizing all of her forces, military and paramilitary. If they had more, they'd cause more damage than they did today. Andrew told David before he dropped the call, "Whatever you have to do, do it quickly and get back to London, there's something you must see yourself."

Roger, standing behind him, let out a sigh, "Why didn't you tell him? That would bring him back home faster."

Andrew answered, "The plan isn't to bring him home, it's to finish the mission. He's on to something already and I have to let him see it through, once he is done, he will come home. I don't want to proceed with Carla's autopsy in his absence, I need him back as it's something he should look at himself."

Roger, with a worried look in his face, told Andrew, "There's nobody on this property, I've searched the entire property and I found no one here. I don't want to think Carla's parents are behind what happened to her, or they are dead but there's a story here that's waiting to unfold itself. I reckon we try to keep them in London, restrict their traveling anyway we can that is if they are trying to leave."

Andrew nodded his head, he tucked his gun in his trouser as he made way for the door. "It's been a roller coaster ride of a day, let's turn in for today, tomorrow we interrogate the attacker's and wait patiently for David's return. He thinks it's a war we can't win but you never win a war by accepting defeat. It might be difficult but battle after battle we come closer to victory, as long as we don't give up, victory will always be in our sights." They left the house, locked the doors as they drove off.

CHAPTER TWENTY-FOUR: HIDEOUT

David could barely sleep that night as he laid down thinking about why Andrew wanted him home so bad, his mind raced to a thousand multiple possibilities. He tried not to get too distracted as his presence was needed where he was. As they rested after a hectic day, Sarah approached him. She could see he had worries, she asked him, "I listened to your call with Andrew, he asked you to come home, that he had a lead on

ISIS, why then are you being awfully worried?"

David looked at her, he sighed as he stood up from the bed, his countenance didn't change despite her presence, "I can't but feel like there's a problem, I've known Andrew a very long time and the way he sounded on the phone suggested there was definitely a problem, he just didn't want me to be too worried that's why he tried to cover it up."

Sarah wanted to cheer him up so he'd focus on their operations the next day, "You can't be too sure, he could just be asking you home because of the giant step he had made in finding ISIS. I mean you said it yourself, he has two of them, once he gets them to talk whereabouts. He'll have the location of Krishikov and we can find that bastard and access the Declon files and the chemical itself, we could stop this once and for all and that I think is what he wanted you to see for yourself."

He appreciated her efforts to make him feel better but he trusted his gut, he knew something was wrong but he wasn't sure what was. He laid down on the bed, this time facing the wall with his back facing Sarah, she wasn't done cheering him up, she asked him, "What do you think the morning holds for us? Are we going to get anything useful there or not?"

David turned slightly facing her, "I hope we do, it's going to be a really risky action, the least that we deserve is something for our efforts, I don't know we'd find anything we need but I really hope we do."

Just at that time, he heard a knock on the door, it was Josh, who came in with a smirk on his face, "I just got off the phone with my weapons guy in Ukraine, the weapons will be ready early tomorrow morning, we leave the motel as early as four a.m. to meet up with him somewhere near the exit of town, pick them up and make our way to the hideout and get on with it. I won't lie to you, but I didn't need Andrew to remind me that I wanted to go home, this horrible country has made an attempt for our lives and now we will go to where they'll make more attempts for our own lives. I want this done so we can get out of here."

Josh waved his hand as he walked out of the door, David looked at Sarah, "You should get some rest yourself, tomorrow is going to be a long day, and you need all the strength you can get."

She looked at him knowing he was only sending her away so he could brood and probably not get a drop of sleep, she stood up from the chair she was sitting and sat by him on the bed, she said to him, "I saw you save people in the worst conditions like you were a superhero or something, I believed in you from that day and I believe in you even now. I don't know how to tell you this but everybody on this team looks up to you, you are our source of strength, seeing you like this is not the best. I need the David I saw at

Larimer, the David I saw earlier today, I need the leader that I want to follow. Brooding doesn't solve problems, the only way to solve them is to make attempt to fix them and if you decide to do that once again, we are here with you, ready and willing to give our lives for the cause. Our lives are in your hands, please don't let it slip." She headed for the door, gently she locked the door as she went to her room.

David turned over and laid on the bed looking upwards, he had a shopping mall red light on in the room, his mind racing, and he thought of all the people he knew and loved. His mind a million places at a time, he started to drift into his thoughts. Memories of his time in Saudi Arabia and in Russia, he thought of himself, the people he had met over time in his life that had led him here. He wanted to speak to Carla, she was his peace and he was lost in thoughts. Maybe she could grant him the peace he needed. He managed sleep, the night was long as he woke up on intervals, restless. He got up once and opened the window, the early morning breeze finding its way into the room, the sounds of the night like sirens called him to his bed. Night's tranquillity talked to him in a voice he couldn't resist. He went back to bed and fell asleep, this time for real.

Gunfire sounded as he dragged himself up, he heard a loud bang on his door as Josh rushed in covered in blood. "Where's Sarah?" he screamed but Josh didn't reply. The rapid sound of an automatic rifle went off, he bent down beside his bed searching his bag to find his hand gun but it wasn't there, he called out to Josh who just stood by the door trembling in fear. "We have to get out of here," he screamed at Josh who still stood frozen like a statue out of fear, he ran towards Josh, held him by the hand. "We have to get out of here." He pulled Josh towards the open window in his room, they found their way down the top floor of the one-story hotel. In no time they were on the ground, they ran for the garage trying to find a car to run away with. They got to the garage, looked around but no car was parked there, he looked at Josh who was still not responsive, Josh was becoming a liability. "You have to snap out of this," he screamed, "else we'll both die here."

Josh gained control as both of them ran from the garage towards the road, taking cover in whatever structure they could find themselves. They ran as quickly as their bodies could allow them, his lungs working beyond its capabilities, the sounds of his feet against the ground really heavy, he pulled Josh the whole way until about four hundred meters into running. Josh regained himself and started to run as well, they ran for a good distance but it seemed the farther they went, the louder the sounds of the gunfire and it was becoming even more rapid. Hiding wasn't an option as the enemies were moving towards them, if they stopped to hide, they'd be found eventually and killed.

They ran continuously until he noticed that Josh wasn't moving as fast as he should be, he looked at Josh and saw blood slipping down his mouth, Josh couldn't say a word but he had been shot multiple times in the back, he fell to the floor as David tried to pull him back up, "Come on man, stay strong, we have to get out of here, I promised you I'd keep you safe and I will, just help me a little and I'll get you to safety."

He tried but Josh could barely respond, he laid on the floor bleeding as he clenched firmly to David's fists, "Save yourself, the fate of Britain rests on your shoulders now, I'll watch over you from where I am."

As David made attempt to run, he saw a hooded man holding an AMG semi-automatic rifle. He stopped, raised his hand in the air, he couldn't see the face as the good and the cover of night protected the man's identity, he pleaded but it fell on deaf ears, the man approached him with every word he spoke to the contrary. He called out to whoever, somebody, anybody but none came to his aid. He saw a woman dressed in hood approaching him as well, she had a gun as well, held firmly in her hand, his heart beating heavily, sweat running down his face, his hand stretched in front of his face as he attempted to block the bullet if he could. The man said to him in a voice he was sure he knew but wasn't able to identify, "Goodbye David, it was a pleasure knowing you." They pulled the trigger, the bullets made contact at the same time he woke up from his bed.

It was a dream. He bent to his side to confirm the time, it was three forty-five a.m., he had to be up and ready in fifteen minutes if he was going to meet up for Josh's plan. He got up from the bed, rushed into the bathroom, obviously worried about the dream, who wanted to kill him he wondered apart from the entire terrorist organization? Those two however didn't feel like terrorists, they knew him like they had mentioned but he didn't know them. He tried to put it away as he prepared himself for the day that waited for him. The pickup site for the weapons was not far off from the hideout that Sarah had identified. She bugged the vehicle she saw at the abandoned Cherishev building not knowing whose it was, that's smart David thought to himself as he got ready. He came out of his room at 3:59 a.m. and saw Josh and Sarah dressed and ready for the mission. Pleased with their preparedness, he didn't have much to say, he just smiled with them as he told them, "Let's do this." They left the hotel and headed for the rental car parked in the garage.

They drove through Zhovkva, in the quiet of night, darkness still covered everywhere, and they could hear the cries of night creatures as they drove through the dark woods, making their way for the pickup point. The lonely road laid in between endless lands that housed trees taller than they'd ever seen, the road, narrow and bent as they drove denied them the opportunity to see what was afar off from them, but its loneliness allowed them a swift travel. In exactly forty-five minutes, they had met with the weapons guy who had a bag of weapons and ammunition ready for them. Josh looked at him with a sick smile on his face when he picked up the bag, he went in immediately going through the inventory. He looked a man possessed as he dropped over guns and explosives.

Sarah looked at him trying to decipher what sort of man he was, he wasn't just an arsonist who wasn't a bad guy but he had love for guns, all she could say was that he was dangerous and it was good he was with them. David looked at the weapons supplier who was not a man of words, David stretched out his hand for a handshake which the man reciprocated but entered into his car and drove away before words were exchanged. David boarded the vehicle, as Josh drove away, he asked him, "How well do you know that guy and trust him?"

Josh replied, "I learnt very early that in this line of work, you trust no one."

They arrived at the base in the cover of night, David parked the vehicle a long way away as the trip prepared themselves for a shopping mall invasion, David wasn't sure what they'd find in the base, but it was a risk worth taking. Engaging in a shootout of this magnitude would have its consequences, so the plan was simple, "Shoot only if you have to but if you don't, stay quiet." David stood behind the car, geared up, wearing a vest before tucking a handgun in his holder. He had a 9mm in his hand and tucked a shopping mall revolver down his boot. Josh, being a lover of a bang, tucked a short gun in his holder as he carried an M-16 in his hand, with multiple blades hidden in different part of his body. Sarah did as she knew how to do best, she picked up an SA80 A2 rifle, the trademark rifle of the British Special Forces.

David looked at her, he smiled as he said to her, "Old habits." She set herself, filling her holder with cartridges, and she tucked her blades down different parts of her body. The trio made way for the base hoping to find the man Igor Krishikov right there and end this madness that was ISIS. They sneaked through the trees, heading straight for the entrance of the base. When they got there, David bent down, his 9mm held firmly in front of his chest, he wasn't sure how to infiltrate the base as he had no prior knowledge, but he hoped to make sense of the situation. With his hand, he drew a square on the floor as he started to explain a plan that he wasn't sure would work, he said, "We are at the entrance, but we can't all infiltrate from one direction, we need to flank them and come in from all sides, that way it gives us the element of surprise. We are going in almost blind, we don't know how many they are, we don't know where they are hiding or where to start searching but we have our wits and guts about us." He looked at Josh who had a smile on his face as always as he continued talking, "They probably have more bodies than us in numbers so try to be as discreet as possible. I am saying that particularly to you Josh, let's avoid the drama, we can't afford to lose anybody."

Josh laughed out loud as he responded, "I have no intentions of dying today, I get the plan, be as quiet as possible but make a sound where absolutely necessary."

That wasn't how he would put it but David knew in his heart that Josh had a problem so he didn't push further, he looked at Sarah who didn't have the same expression as Josh as he told her, "Don't you worry, you just heard him say he wasn't ready to die, I'm not either, I have a wife and two kids to be with, dying is not an option. You just have to lay low, strike when you have to and I promise you it'll be fine." She nodded her head as David told them before they set out, "I don't think there's much of them there, even if there is, they are still out, you can tell by the lack of activity in the base. We got this."

The trio parted ways trying to access the base from different directions, the base was barricaded by a mesh fence and they could see what went on inside and for a terrorist stronghold, it was rather inactive. David made his entrance not far from the main gate, cutting the fence gently with a snip as he made his way into the base, he saw three men stationed at the main gate, but they were pretty out of commission, he made his foray as quiet as possible reducing drastically his sound, he had on his gun a sound suppressor as did Sarah and Josh. They all had on FPN surveillance pieces on their ears so they could communicate with each other. David had predicted that whoever meant something in this camp had to be in here somewhere. The base was empty as he saw not more than ten men positioned strategically in the base, the lack of security gave him the impression that nothing valuable was here. He headed for the main building with the intention of finding Krishikov.

The entrance to the building was unguarded, as he forayed deep into the building, he could hear voices, and people were inside. He sneaked through the open doors he found on the hallway until he got to a sort of lobby where he saw three men unarmed with one sitting on a chair in a corner in the room. David tapped the device on his ear as he spoke to either Josh or Sarah, "Are you in? I'm looking at some kingpin or something, I am going to engage, I need back up."

No response came for a second, he was already worried when Sarah replied, "I just made my way through three men, I managed to put them out of commission, where are you, I'm heading your way now."

He sighed in relief when Josh also responded, "They aren't ready for us, I just put seven out of commission, I've made my way around the camp, there's no more men standing guard, headed for the only permanent structure in the base."

David responded immediately, "I'm in the building, I'm looking at the leader of the base, there's not much in here in terms of security, just four men without guns, I'll engage but I need you here ASAP." David came out of hiding with his gun pointing at the man sitting in the chair, he shouted at the top of his voice, probably not the best decision he had made, his shout attracted others who probably were in the building ran out with rifles in their hands, he ran back into hiding as they opened fire. The sounds of the gunshots filled the air astounds after rounds hit the wall where

David was hiding, he touched the device as he spoke to Josh and Sarah, "Where's that back up, you can hear the gunshots right? I'm the one they are shooting at, I can't hold on lads, I need you." He brought out his hand from his hiding spot as he shot back with no real target in mind. For every round he shot, they shot dozens more.

They approached him, shooting sporadically as he couldn't come out from hiding, they provided cover for him as they headed towards him, he changed his cartridge as he awaited his miracle, they were less than a foot away from him, one of them in a heavily accented voice spoke up, "We have you surrounded, come out and die quickly, stay hiding and we will come over and kill you slowly and painfully."

David replied, "I'll take my chance with slowly and painfully." He kissed his gun, as he raised his head, he saw Josh and Sarah positioned with their rifles ready to fire. He smiled as he asked them, "What took you so long?"

The voice responded, "I was going to kill you slowly and painfully either way." As the terrorists charged at him, Sarah and Josh opened fire sporadically. David sat still, his hands on his ears as they continued shooting for a while. The terrorists fell on the floor, David ran towards the lobby as the kingpin he had seen made way for the exit, David signalled Josh to flank him.

David followed him on foot, he ran dropping things on the way as he passed, David avoided them and chased after him not wanting to give him even an ounce of space between them. He made for the exit door and was turning around the building to head for the exit when he ran straight into Josh's fist. The collision was fatal, he fell to the love, three of his teeth in the air. He held on to his mouth as blood gushed out. David approached him lying helplessly on the floor with his hand over his mouth, as David approached him to ask questions, he brought out a knife from his pocket as he slit his own throat. David got there as did Sarah, Josh was already standing over his dead body. David shook his head, "He'd rather die than tell us what he knows about Declon 5?" David searched his pocket and found his wallet, his card read Denis Krishikov. He continued talking, "Krishikov, any relation to Igor?"

Sarah walked up to the body as she ducked in front of the dead man, "What sick individual introduces their own blood relatives to a life like this? What was he thinking? Killing himself? I can never really understand these people"

David smiled as he told them, "Zhovkva didn't deliver to us what we expected, we saw something but it bore no fruit, it's now back to Andrew and Roger back at London, they have two in custody, we have to go back and see what we can pick up from there." David snapped the body lying on the floor as he sent the picture to a secure number that they were given to report progress, he called the number and immediately it answered, he spoke, "This is special agent David Scarlet, I just sent over a picture, I need you to run facial recognition and send back to me ASAP. We might have made a bit of a mess in Ukraine and we are headed out of Ukraine this morning, we'll be in Britain later today."

The response he got was, "Affirmative to all directives, see you soon agent."

As they left the base for where their car was parked, David received an email from MI6, containing information about Denis Krishikov, he looked at it keenly as Roger drove the car, he told them, "Denis Krishikov is English, the man who just committed suicide is English, not English by descent but English by birth, born to Yuri and Ariana Krishikov, it is said he had a brother of whom we have no record but I reckon it has to be Igor Krishikov, the same man we are searching for. I am a little confused, it says here that the entire family is English, and the parents died a long time ago. Why would they be English, and they spearhead an organization to destroy Britain?"

Sarah responded, "We have to go back to Britain, I can't but feel like there's nothing her for us to find, like Andrew mentioned, Britain, that's where it'd end." They boarded the vehicle as they drove off of Zhovkva headed back to the airport in a bid to board a flight back to London.

CHAPTER TWENTY-FIVE:
HEARTBREAK

The day began like every other, the sun rose just beyond the stretch of sea, the birds sang their ever so gentle song, the day took over control from the night as people went about their days work. Andrew could barely sleep as he had been awake the entire night, he sort a way to break the news to David about the demise of his wife and the disappearance of his in-laws who looked like suspects in his wife's death. He got up to prepare himself to go back to MI6 HQ to investigate the men he had arrested. He had managed to keep words of their arrest a secret so Igor Krishikov or whoever wouldn't find out they were in police custody. He was about to head out when his phone rang, it was the director of the GCHQ, he picked up in a hurry to hear the director select his words carefully, "Igor contacted us last night, he wanted to congratulate us on our success at

Kensington and at Hyde Park, he mentioned however that we have three days left before he begins to use the Declon 5 he had stolen from our bio-lab. He was kind enough to demonstrate the potency of the Declon 5, injecting a lethal dose into the streams of an innocent man, who died a quick yet gruesome death. I tell you this to remind you that time is of the essence. What do you have on the lads you arrested, we need all the information we can collect if we are to stop them."

Andrew answered, "We haven't interrogated them yet sir, there was an incident last night that we had to attend to, the attack at the women's health clinic. I'm on my way to MI6 HQ right about now and I will interrogate them myself. I promise to get back to you with whatever information I can extract from them."

The director seemed impatient as he wanted the case closed quickly, he replied, "Do that fast, we don't have all the time in the world."

The call dropped before Andrew could say anything and as he tucked his phone in his pocket, it rang again. It was Roger who seemed enthusiastic. Andrew told him, "You seem pretty happy today lad, is there something I should be happy about as well?"

Roger replied, "I have been with the terrorists all night, I couldn't sleep so I went early to interrogate them, they gave me a name, one Harry Dickens, you have to get here as soon as you can."

Andrew had questions, but he believed he could ask them better when he got there. He drove to HQ as fast as he could and in no time he had arrived. He rushed into the interrogation chamber but on his way there, he met Roger seating on a bench just in the hallway, "What is it lad? You didn't sleep at all over the night?"

Roger responded, "Sleep? I couldn't, I worried a lot about the fate of Britain, knowing well that the deadline was fast approaching, I had to get answers and I got something. I walked into the interrogation room where I met them both seated afraid for their lives, they are just kids, they are not even aware the magnitude of their offense. I separated them into different rooms where I quizzed them separately. I employed the methods of something called the prisoners dilemma, I learned from one of my cases, turns out I didn't need it anyways as they gave me what I wanted with little hassle. They don't know much but this Harry Dickens guy seems to know something, we find him, we can find Igor."

Andrew was really impressed with what Roger had achieved on his own, "Bravo lad, you are quite the agent, I got a call from the director earlier today, the deadline isn't in a week anymore, it's in three days, they got a call from Igor Krishikov himself and he told them that, so whoever this Harry Dickens guy is, we have to find him immediately and end this before the Declon 5 is released into Britain. That is one thing we should prevent from happening at all cost. This Harry Dickens, what did they tell you about him?"

"They said he took boys in from a young age, he raises them in a yard off the south West End of London, they said, just recently, he was approached by a Russian or something of the sort to recruit some of the boys and he obliged, they have no real skill with the gun Andrew, that's why it was easy to take them down like we did." Andrew knew at that point that Roger felt it too, the pain of cutting down young English lads at Kensington. Roger continued, "Not all of them were but the ones in the room with the foreign secretary at Kensington, they were English lads, weren't they?"

Andrew nodded his head remorsefully as he replied, "They were, I noticed it too, and I was hoping you wouldn't just so you don't go through what I went through."

"This animal starts a terrorist organization and recruits English kids to fight their home and have us kill our own for his cause? We have to put him down."

The odds were in their favour, find this Dickens guy and find Krishikov, Andrew thought to himself, they were just about to leave HQ when a call came in, it was the director, he wanted a word with Andrew and Roger. The pair rushed into his office hoping to round up in time and head out to Bloomsbury where Dickens resides. They hurried into his office where he sat behind a desk, a cigar in his mouth, he was alone and had not much lighting in his office, he had two chairs facing his as he gestured for them to sit which they did. He started to talk, "What did you get from the terrorists you arrested? I got wind you wanted to interrogate them yourself and I'm guessing you have, well what did they say?"

Andrew intervened, "They gave us a name, one Harry Dickens, we are about to go look it up."

The director stood up from his chair, "David got something in Ukraine although they made a mess that we had to clean up, it wasn't tangible however as the only suspect they had committed suicide. I need updates, whenever and wherever. I told you earlier that they had cut short the time they gave and we have just two days to find the Declon else we'd count our dead. You can use whatever you want, please, just find them."

Andrew nodded his head as the pair got up to leave the office. He was just at the door when the director signalled them as he said, "Lest I forget to tell you, David and the others will be back in London in an hour or two, bring them up to speed and do whatever you have to."

Andrew and Roger left, heading straight for Bloomsbury, it was nine forty-five, the day was bright, and people going about their lives not knowing the threat that stood before them. Roger looked at every cluster of people as he'd sigh once he saw a gathering. Andrew looked at him, feeling his pain said to him, "We will sort this out and they don't have to die, don't be too troubled." Roger brought out his gun and checked his rounds as they drove down their busy road. They approached the address they were given, a house stood quiet in the suburbs of London. They walked towards the door, expecting a full house but yet again in two nights, the house looked and felt deserted, Andrew approached the building from the front door as usual as Roger went behind. It was quiet but while Andrew put his foot on the front porch, he heard sounds in the house like falling plates. Roger was stationed out back to ensure whoever was in didn't escape through the back door but as he stood, he saw a man jump out one of the windows on the side of the building, Roger shouted to give Andrew signal as he made chase after the fleeing man.

The running man knew the area well and gave Roger a run for his money, Andrew ran back to the vehicle as he followed via the car. The man ran in between houses, running into some open doors in a bid to slow Roger down, he avoided obstacles like he had been running his entire life but Roger was no slouch, he followed him, matching him stride for stride, not wanting to allow him out of his site. Andrew remained in the car, driving as fast as he could as he saw them dash through the buildings. The man jumped over a fence, Roger made attempts too but couldn't, he stood there laughing at Roger with the idea that he had escaped but he was brought back to reality when he heard a gun cocking just behind his head. He looked behind him and there stood Andrew without a smile on his face, ready to knock the breaks out of the man if need be.

He raised his hands up, not wanting to see if Andrew would shoot or not, the expression on Andrew's face gave the impression that he'd shoot.

"Don't shoot, I'm innocent of whatever you are charging me off, I didn't do anything," he cried but Andrew would have none of it.

He had him in handcuffs, sitting on the floor, "You are Harry Dickens, aren't you?"

Roger had made his way around the fence and saw Harry sitting on the floor with cuffs, he smiled as he said to Harry, "Serves you right if you are innocent as you say, why did you run?"

Harry looked at himself and at Andrew and Roger, "Look at me lads, coppers would arrest me at first glance, I look really suspicious mate." Roger smiled.

Andrew asked, "What do you know about a man named Igor Krishikov, you best tell me what you know, I'm not in a good place right now, once I get wind you are lying to me, I'm going to shoot you in the face."

Harry immediately became worried as he tried to explain himself, "I don't know an Igor Krishikov, if this is about the boys, I was approached by some man about the boys I've been keeping. Yes, I pick these boys up from the street when they have nowhere to go, I keep them safe, feed and give them a place to sleep, often times, I send them out to steal and earn a living for themselves and me. That's all I do, I don't know a Krishikov or whatever you call him."

Roger cut in, "So you want us to believe you don't know the man who you gave the boys to? And you don't know why they came for them? You must be joking. You best be talking else I'm going to look away for a brief second and my partner is going to do to you as he pleases."

Harry looked at Andrew who still wasn't smiling and decided to take his chance with Roger, he started talking, "I don't know them by their names as they didn't introduce themselves with their names, he came to me some time ago and said something about his boss wanting some of the lads, I asked around from a few contacts I had and I was told something about a guy who was Russian or Ukrainian or something like that recruiting lads for some big test or something. Some people said he was English and others didn't, I don't know, he was scary and I never asked, I just handed the lads over and took my money."

Andrew angrily kicked him, "So you sold the kids that weren't yours. You might not be part of the master plan, but you will face the judgment for your own offenses."

Harry tried to defend himself, "I know I messed up selling kids but what's a guy like me with nothing do to survive?"

Andrew was going to respond to him when his phone rang, it was David. "Hey Andy, I'm in London, heading for GCHQ, let's meet up, there's a lot we have to talk about." Andrew agreed as he dragged Harry up into the car as they drove off.

The drive back to HQ was a long one but it was even longer as Andrew thought to himself how he was going to break the news of Carla's death to David and the fact that neither Kim nor Carla's parents had been seen the past two days, he drove as fast he could with Harry constantly pleading for his release the whole ride there. He came down and handed Harry to the officers on duty. He headed straight for the briefing room where he saw David, Sarah and Josh, he went straight to David as he hugged him dearly, Roger came in as well, exchanging his pleasantries, he tried to avoid eye contact with David as did Andrew. David could feel the tension in both of them, he was starting to get worried, and he tried to establish communication as he asked Andrew, "What is your update in London?"

Andrew sighed as he hesitated to say anything, David snarled at him, "If there is a problem, I reckon you start talking."

Roger made an attempt to walk out of the office as he couldn't stay there when the information was broken to David, but David refused him exit, "You stand there until he has said what he has to say."

Andrew finally mustered the courage to speak, "Yesterday was a really busy day for all of us at HQ, the coppers, the military and all, we had three attacks simultaneously and while we knew about two, we were completely oblivious of the third one, we only found out after it had happened."

David cut in, "We don't have all day mate, our deadlines just in front of us, a week if I'm right."

Andrew continued, "Three days, it was just reviewed by Krishikov. As I was saying, the third attack was at the Women's Health Clinic Dulwich."

David froze as he heard the place, he said to them, "That's the same hospital, Carla was admitted."

Andrew nodded his head as he continued talking, "There were five casualties in total, one of which was your wife Carla."

David froze as he heard the words, he tried to hold his dismay, but he couldn't, his legs couldn't hold his body as he sought for a chair to rest his withered legs, he sat down, no words as tears began to roll down his cheeks, he asked Andrew, "How did it happen?"

"I got there for situation report and I saw her corpse, every other body had bullet wounds all over but hers didn't, the doctors think she died of a shock bearing in mind her constant pregnancy complications." David wasn't convinced as he asked Andrew and Roger, "I have to ask this and I need you two to be completely honest with me, do you believe she died of shock or she was murdered?" A sudden silence filled the air as neither Andrew nor Roger responded, everybody remained quiet until David shouted as loud as his lungs could carry him, "Answer me, dang it!!"

Andrew responded, "We have no evidence to believe she was murdered and the events that transpired on the day of the attacks were fierce, it made absolute sense that it was a shock. I know processing this is going to be hard for you, but you have to, I'm sorry for your loss and I had her body kept at London General not allowing the doctors to run an autopsy on her without your permission." David was crying, tears pouring out of his eyes as he remembered the memories of his wife and thought of his unborn kid.

David appreciated the gesture as he stood up from the chair, Andrew and Roger got close to him on either side to make sure he was stable as Andrew continued, "There's more bad news David, Mark, Laura and Kim, they have been missing since the attack yesterday, we went to your house and Mark's but we couldn't find them, the worst part of it now is I can't tell if Mark and Laura ran away or we're kidnapped or killed as well. The scene at their apartment felt like they went away in a hurry, but I couldn't believe that because why would they when their daughter just died, they'd always been by her side, they ought to have been there, but I don't know where they are and trust me, I've searched everywhere for them." David could hardly stand anymore, he didn't know where to start from, he sat down yet again as he tried to process his thoughts.

He was about to start wailing when Roger said something that caught his attention and gave him reason to go on, Roger shouted at him, "I might be wrong but I think Carla's death and her parents and your kid's disappearance has something to do with ISIS, I don't think Carla was killed in the line of fire like everybody else that died, I think she was killed because she is involved with you, I don't know, I might be wrong but I want you to know that I think if we solve Carla's death, we get the information we need on ISIS plus I need you, you are an inspiration to me, to Sarah, to Josh, to every young agent out there looking to make a mark on Britain, I fear Carla's demise might put you down but please don't let it, please, let's end this and get revenge for Carla."

David stood up from where he sat down, he went straight to Roger who stood there looking at him, David pat him on the shoulder, "Thank you lad, this might be the worst news I have ever heard in my life but I'm sure Carla would want me to find Kim and Mark and Laura and save Britain.

Andrew, take me to her corpse, she is going to help us solve this case even in her death. Roger, contact Women's Health Clinic Dulwich. You and Sarah, head down there and get me CCTV tapes, I need to see who went in and out of her room and when, Josh, go with them and keep them safe. We are going to get to the bottom of this."

Andrew looked at Roger and David as he said to Roger, "I told you he'd get over it in no time, its David, and it's what he does."

CHAPTER TWENTY-FIVE:
A STEP CLOSER

Andrew and David left HQ as they headed for London General, as they drove, David remained silent, not knowing what to say, a lot was going wrong, but he had to stay strong for his team, Roger had put his faith in him, and he had to pay him back with results. He finally said words to Andrew as he asked him, "Do you think Roger is right? Did Carla die because she was married to me?"

Andrew answered, "I'd like to think not, yet you are more closely tied to ISIS than many others, but I don't think they killed Carla to get to you, I still want to believe she died of shock and not that she was murdered or anything."

David looked at him keenly as he spoke, "You don't believe that. You said something about Mark and Laura leaving in a hurry, what was that about?"

Andrew answered him, "After we saw Carla's body, knowing fully well that you were out of the country, we opted to inform her parents but when we got there, the house was deserted, clothes on the floor in the bedroom like the occupants of the house just got up and left in a hurry. The TV was on, the kitchen tap was running as well, it was either they ran away or there were kidnapped or maybe even killed, that's how it looked. I'm not saying they killed their daughter, I mean I've seen how close they are and I know first-hand they wouldn't do that but I just wanted to let you know. Once we are done with Carla, we can go back there so you can see for yourself, besides what are you going to do with Carla's body?

David answered, "I am going to run a full autopsy, find out if my wife died of shock or something else killed her. I can't just sit idly by and allow her killer go free."

Andrew sighed as he said, "You seem pretty convinced that she was murdered?"

"Not yet but I intend to find out and find out soon."

They arrived at London General Morgue, they had GCHQ forensic team with them.

David didn't know how to feel, he tried to think of the possibility of a mistake that it wasn't Carla but someone else but he knew Andrew couldn't mistake his wife for someone else. He was quiet the whole time as they went in, the attendant brought the corpse out and it dawned on him that it was no mistake, it was Carla, he got close to her as the tears rolled down yet again. His feet trembled as his breath hastened, he looked at his wife, the woman he had loved forever, lying lifeless. His job exposed him to the possibility of death more than a lot of people but still he wasn't dead, Carla was faraway from danger or so he thought but she was the one lying lifeless in a morgue. He was filled with emotions, he wasn't sure if he was to be sad or angry at the time, a part of him didn't want to let her go but at the same time, another part of him wanted so bad to leave the morgue and find out who did this to her and have his revenge. He also had the feeling of concern and worry about the whereabouts of Kim, Mark and Laura. He looked at her closely one last time as he signalled the forensic scientists to do their jobs. He looked at Andrew who came closer to him as they walked out of the morgue. His phone rang, it was Roger who said to him, "We've got the footage and it promises to be really interesting, we'll meet you at HQ in thirty. We might with this footage, find out who and where Igor Krishikov is." David smiled half-heartedly as he commended their efforts, he walked to the car, looking at the ambulance as it drove away with Carla's remains, he wiped his face, he wasn't over his pain, but he knew what came foremost in his heart, finding Kim and then having his revenge.

David and Andrew headed back to HQ to meet Josh, Sarah and Roger. The drive back was quiet, he said nothing to Andrew and Andrew said nothing to him. David's thought rested on how he was going to find his wife's killer and also find Kim. Andrew would occasionally look at him, feeling his pain and wishing he could help him solve his problem but there was nothing he could do other than follow procedure and conduct investigations like David intended. They got back to HQ, meeting the others in the entrance as they all went straight in to review the tapes. Roger quickly told David as they walked in, "I don't know what to exactly make of the tapes I saw but I don't think it was shock, just about the time she was proclaimed dead, a strange man walked into her room, it was during the attack and he wasn't even carrying a gun, he walked past all the terrorists with none doing anything to him so I think he's one of them but you should see it yourself and come up with what you think happened." David said no words as he walked even faster, he needed to be sure what was going on and he needed to take sentiments away from this case as that would cloud his judgments and bring him closer to death than he had ever been.

While in the room, Roger brought out a USB flash drive and inserted it into a computer as it displayed a folder in a large screen that stood in front of all of them, he looked at Andrew, David and the rest of the team as he saw in them the eagerness to see what he had brought for them, he said to David, "More work would be needed after we go through this tape but I can guarantee you that whatever you see here will go a long way to helping us close this case." David sat upright wanting to see what was recorded on the flash, thoughts of Carla swept through his mind as his blood rushed all over his body, his heart pounding more than a parade drum as he held firmly to his table. Andrew looked at him as he saw the hate in his face for whoever was to appear on the TV. Roger went straight for the supercomputer that served as the keyboard, mouse and the CPU but stood a few feet wide like a table in the centre of the room.

He browsed through the system trying to access the folder for the video that had saved on the flash, he could tell from the tension in the room that David was growing impatient as was the rest of them, he opened the file and in it, they found the video that Roger had recorded from the women's health clinic. He opened it, skipping through the scenes he regarded as unnecessary, he stopped skipping when he saw a man dressed in a jacket and a baseball cap walked through the lobby of the clinic. He pointed at the man and said to his teammates as they sat patiently watching for what would happen next. Amidst the attack, the man walked through streams of terrorists, none questioning him, he went straight for the hallway, stopping often to exchange words with the armed men that stood in the lobby. Roger told the rest of them that watched keenly, "Look at that man, he's the last person to be seen entering into Carla's room but something else stands out in the clip, something I know you wouldn't like. I mentioned it earlier that Carla's death had something to do with ISIS and it is evident in this footage. It seemed like on the day, Carla and the foreign secretary were the targets."

David didn't understand why his pregnant wife would be a target for a terrorist organization, he asked Roger, "Why would Carla be a target? What harm could she cause them being heavily pregnant and even if she wasn't pregnant, she wasn't a threat of any kind to them?"

Andrew looked at David, "Like Roger said, it could have been a statement to you, to make you stay off the case."

Roger continued, "I thought so too earlier but I highly doubt it now, I don't think it was a statement to you or anybody, the events that followed creates the impression that Carla's parents have some sort of involvement with ISIS. Where'd you say they were from again?"

David looked at Roger with uncertainty, "Are you saying my wife's parents have something to do with ISIS? Come to think of it, they've always said they had ancestry from some other European country, but that means nothing, it doesn't make them terrorists, it could have been a coincidence or something, keep playing. I'll find that out myself."

Roger leaned forward as he touched a button on the keyboard as the tape continued playing. The strange man walked through the chaos with no one obstructing or stopping him, he made his way through to the hallway, a few meters away from Carla's room, he had managed to walk through the clinic without the CCTV cameras picking his face, he entered a room which happened to be Carla's room. He stayed there for almost ten minutes before coming out of the room, just in front of the camera, he raised his head as the camera picked just a glimpse of his right cheek, his tattoo that was drawn to look like two drops of water stood out as Roger screenshot him as he adjusted his cap.

Roger dragged the screenshot as he displayed it on the top right corner of the screen. He continued the video showing the strange man walking away and shortly after, Carla's parents walking through the swarm of terrorists with no one paying attention to them as they walked out of the clinic without obstruction from the terrorists. "This is where I have a problem, I know you might not want to see it the way I do but it looks the only way to see it. Mark and Laura probably have some sort of relationship with ISIS, maybe Carla found out and was killed for it, there's no other logical explanation than that one. I know you don't believe me, but it looks the truth," said Roger as he walked towards David.

Andrew cut in, "The tapes don't show us what happened inside the room, we cannot be sure they killed her, she could have died of shock like the doctor said."

"You don't believe that, do you Andrew?" David asked, his voice not able to go louder, the burden on his heart was heavy and all could see he needed to let himself free from the pain he was carrying. The love of his life and the mother of his unborn child had most likely been murdered by the people she trusted the most and he could do nothing about it. He continued talking as his voice managed to increase, "I cannot say for certain they killed her because truly we didn't see what transpired in the room, hence the need for the autopsy report once that comes out, we'd know if she actually died of shock or was murdered." He looked at Andrew who was careful with his words, he wasn't familiar with what David was going through, but he knew all too well the pain of loss. David told him, "I know you are saying this with my best interest at heart, but I can't help but admit that Roger is right, finding Carla's killer can also help us find the Declon 5 files and the hierarchy of ISIS."

Roger nodded his head as he walked back towards the screen, "There's more to the tapes but it hits a dead end shortly after, our mystery man walks out of the clinic into a black Bentley from what we could gather, we could see a shopping mall portion of the car but the number plates wasn't accessible. I know this is not the way you wanted the footage to end but I'm afraid this is where it stops, I can't figure out more, but I reckon if we work together, something might come up."

David looked at his wristwatch, it was already late at night, he signalled Andrew touching his wristwatch as he said, "We should turn in for the day, I reckon we are pretty tired, yeah? I know we all want to solve this mystery and end all this ISIS nonsense once and for all but we can't do that if we don't get all the rest we can. Tomorrow might be the last day we have before the attack on London with the Declon 5 but I believe that we'd get this done, I appreciate you all for all you've done over the past few days but it's not done, we still have a lot to do before we can finally rest easy but I trust in your abilities and believe that together, we can end this." He got up to leave but no one moved an inch, he looked around with every member of the team, looking back at him unwilling to go home. Perplexed, he asked, "What madness is this?"

Andrew stood up, walked towards David, his hands on David's shoulder told him, "I believe I speak on behalf of everyone sitting here when I say, we can't go home, we can't sleep next to our wives and our loved ones when we know Britain is at risk, when we know the lives of our loved ones is in danger, when we know you have no one to go back to. We didn't get involved to sleep when we are close to the end, we are here to work round the clock to ensure that all is well for when we eventually solve this and find the Declon 5 files, we can sleep as long as we want. As for me, I will take time off, to Maldives or some tropical resort and have the time of my life but till then David, right here by your side, fighting ISIS is where I want to be." One by one they all stood up, surrounding David rendering to his ears word of support. Emotions grew strong within David but as a leader, he had to maintain composure as he looked at his teammates.

"Thank you all very much, it's almost midnight but I reckon we are going to be awake all day, Josh, Sarah I need you to go ask some questions to our friends in the cell, I think there's more they are going to tell us tonight, Andrew you are with me, we are going to go through this video as many times as possible until we find something here that shows us a path to follow. We are getting this done." They left, attending to their various assignments. Hours passed,

Josh, Sarah and Roger locked in the interrogation room asked questions after questions, but answers weren't forthcoming. David and Andrew looking at the videos found nothing. The trio came out from the room to report their lack of success to David who, alongside David, still paid close attention to the videos.

Looking at the video with some conviction, Josh said as casually as he always does, "It's a rental car."

Everybody looked at him, David was curious as to why he had that opinion, "Why would you say that Josh?"

He smiled as he walked to the keyboard and zoomed out the car, still smiling he said, "It's Ethan Holland car rentals, that's his logo on the rear windshield of the vehicle." Roger immediately checked to confirm, he took control of the keyboard as he checked Ethan Holland on Google and alas, it was a rental car from Ethan Holland.

Roger, out of joy, hugged Josh, "You crazy arsonist, you just blew our case wide open. How did you know it was Ethan Holland rental?"

Josh laughed, "I rented a car there when I did my first wedding and I used one yet again when I was undercover a while ago. I've done business with them a lot of time so I should know."

Reprieved they had a link, David told everyone, "We've gotten somewhere today, we rest for tomorrow we have to go out to the rentals and see what we can find from there. We also receive the forensic reports and we can tell from there what we are looking at. Good work lads, go get some much-needed rest."

CHAPTER TWENTY-SIX:
CONFIRMED

They dispersed as the night went into the quiet beginnings of the day, each slept in whatever space they could find. David however struggled to find peace enough to shut his eyes. His failures to protect his family made the night unbearable. He would often find himself slipping into the firm embrace of his thoughts, not good thoughts but the fierce grips of his worst nightmares. He could hear Carla calling in the abyss of darkness, he'd chase after her drowning voice, but he was unable to pinpoint her location. Alone in a vast open space with no light to illuminate his very steps, he fared poorly as he could neither behold nor touch his beloved. He'd open his eyes every now and then, but his fears lived with him in reality as much as they did in his own thoughts. He got up, hoping to find any ounce of peace in the quietness of the dark and silent night but there, rested even more worries for him. He thought to himself, often allowing words slip from his mouth. Life as he knew it was gone. Even if he survived the ISIS attack, he had no reason to live. He laid down yet again on his bed and his thoughts as if to give him reason to live, reminded him of Kim. He stood up, worried of her whereabouts. He had no choice, Carla was dead, and Mark and Laura seemed more like suspects than they are victims. Kim was the only one oblivious of what was going on and she was too young a child to make any attempt to communicate with him, he had to do something to find her.

As he stood up to take a stroll, Andrew stood up beside him, "I know it's not easy expecting you to act like nothing happened when we know everything happened but I want you to know one thing, we are behind you, we'll help you with whatever you need and we'll find your baby girl." David turned behind him and saw Andrew, Andrew walked up to him, place his right hand on David's right shoulder.

David nodded as he headed towards the window, "I told you something when I was in Ukraine about ISIS. It's not an organization that we can put down once and for all, I feel stopping this attack now will just delay them."

Andrew asked, "You mentioned that the other time, what do you mean?"

David sighed as he faced Andrew, "At Ukraine, we were attacked by a team of men we didn't know and didn't know how they knew us, we arrived at Zhovkva and headed to the address that we were given but ISIS had already infiltrated and killed our target, we tried to hold back the ISIS agent but we couldn't get a hold of him as he escaped, in a very short time, a swarm of ISIS operatives were already there trying to put us out. They have support, they have youth, they have widespread, ISIS is only just beginning, stopping them here will amount to just slowing them down but if they can brainwash even English lads, they are obviously going to keep growing."

"What do you reckon we do?"

"I'm not sure, I don't even know what we are going to do to avert the current problem we are having. Once this is done, it becomes a counter terrorism issue. I just hope that like other terrorist groups, the rest of the world join hands together to fight them because I fear it might become too big and too hard just for Britain."

Andrew sighed as he walked away from David to get some rest, "Rest up brother, we have a long day in front of us, tomorrow. We need you in full strength." David agreed as he forced himself to sleep. He was awake for a while before eventually giving in to his tiredness.

Roger was up before anyone else, he had gone back to all the files they had gathered over the weeks on the ISIS case. Flipping through papers, he searched like he had misplaced something and needed to find it as quickly as possible. Josh joined him shortly after, "A little eager, are we?"

He looked back and saw Josh sitting, "We don't have a lot of time on our hands anymore. They strike in one day, we need to at least have something to pursue if we plan to stop them."

As they were talking, they heard David's voice, "Roger, Josh, I need you to go with Sarah to Mark and Laura's, I still think there's something for you to see there, Andrew you go with me to Ethan Holland to ask a few questions. It's the final day as the day of reckoning is tomorrow. Don't be overly pressured, we'll fix it all today, I guarantee you that."

David checked his wristwatch, it was five a.m., they wouldn't meet up with Ethan Holland this early in the morning, he needed to wait for Carla's results. As they sat down, deliberating on the course of action, the forensic scientist walked in with a file in his hand, he walked straight to David who seemed pretty shocked that she hadn't gone home the previous day, she got to him as she handed him the file, she said to him, "I could tell you what I found or you could read it yourself from the file, which would you prefer?" David looked at her as he told her to go on. She looked at him with a worried expression, "Your wife Carla didn't die of shock, I think she was murdered." She paused to allow David a little time to digest what she had just said. He placed his hands on his forehead as he rested on the table that stood not far away from him. She continued talking, "Looking through her organs, the lungs had a dark coloration, it's typical of people who had inhaled something toxic but checking within, we couldn't find anything harmful in her respiratory tract, she had multiple organ failure, but I believe, it began with her respiratory tract. Whatever went into her system, damaged her respiratory system before venturing to cause further damage. Since it wasn't inhaled, we are checking with toxicology to see if it was swallowed but results aren't out yet. We are trying on our end to see if it was injected because it wasn't inhaled and ingested. Your wife's death is not necessarily a mystery but what was used is a mystery, but I want to guarantee you that once the result comes from toxicology, we will be able to ascertain the cause of death."

David and the rest of his team suspected that Carla probably was the first victim of the Declon 5 but why she was killed was the mystery. Roger, Sam and Josh left HQ immediately, the doctor had finished speaking to Mark's apartment, David looked at Andrew who stood behind him, he responded to the doctor, "Thank you for your assistance, I need her covered as soon as you can." He sat down on the chair as he tried to find his sense of coordination, "I can't help but think she was killed because of me."

Andrew replied, "Nobody was supposed to know we were in charge of the ISIS case if it hadn't gone the way it did."

David cut in, "But they do and that have cost me the life of my wife and my kid, this is bollocks, I have to find out who did this and why." He went into the lab with the doctor to take one look at Carla before he went out to find her killer. He stood there as he clenched her cold fist with his hand, the baby had been extracted from her and had been buried earlier. Thoughts ran through his mind as he held on to her. "It should have been me, you didn't have to pay the price for my involvement with ISIS, I'd have gladly given my life for yours? I'm sorry I couldn't take care of you, I never got to see the baby. We'll never have one of those moments we always wanted together. I failed you and I apologize. The most I can do now is find whoever did this to you and bring them to justice. Until we meet again, stay where you are and wait for me."

He left the lab and met Andrew who stood at the garage waiting for him, they left in Andrew's car as they set out to Ethan Holland mega car station. The drive took no time as the roads were empty, it was a Saturday morning and not many people were out. They arrived at the car dealership complex, it was a marvel. The building made of transparent glass, it hadn't opened for the day but its staff filled the structure. Spectacles in the name of vehicles stood on display as David walked in, jaws dropped for the marvel that Ethan's cars. They walked in spinning round as they couldn't get enough of the beauty of the building.

The sounds of a voice reporter filled the air as it awakened staffs to their respective duty posts, David and Andrew headed straight for the office complex, a shopping mall elevator stood at the side of the building which took them upstairs. The security had made attempts to stop them, but they couldn't when they identified as law enforcement.

The elevator got to its floor and when it opened, they saw a woman who had a file in her hand, she said to them, "Hi, I'm Lauren, I reckon you came to see Mr. Holland?" David nodded his head as the lady continued, "This way gentlemen," they followed still sucking up the wonders of engineering that was Ethan's complex. They walked to an office door as they stood, the lady knocked gently, and they heard a voice from inside the office that ushered them in which they obeyed. David and Andrew walked in and the office was more than they had ever entered. Its interior decor stood amongst the finest they had ever beheld in their life. The details mapped to perfection. In front of them, stood a table and chair so marvellously designed and polished that it just should be added to one of the wonders of the world. David tried to maintain his cool as he approached the desk.

"You must be Mr. Ethan Holland? Forgive us for interrupting your busy schedule so early but we have a few questions that we need you to answer. Once you do that for me, we are out of your skin, I promise."

Ethan hesitated as he asked politely, "Can I get you kind gentlemen anything?"

David cut in not wanting any distractions, "No thank you, if you would just answer a few questions and show us a few things, we'd be out of here in next to no time."

Ethan relaxed into his chair as he reached for a cigar, "Why ask on then."

David sat upright, "Thank you very much sure. The questions are really direct, do you know any Igor Krishikov?"

Ethan puffed out smoke. He had his wits with him as he was calm as possible, "Asking about others without introducing yourself, that isn't a very gentleman thing to do."

David smiled as he started all over again, "I'm David Scarlet and my partner is Andrew Charlton and we are with the metropolitan police, we just want to ask you a few questions and nothing else." Ethan smiled as he nodded his head, David continued, "We are investigating the recent attacks and wanted to know your involvements with a certain Igor Krishikov? Do you know him?"

Ethan looked at them keenly, his cigar still clutched between his index finger and his thumb as he rolled his chair in a semicircle, "Never heard of him."

David, not sure if to believe him or not, brought out a picture that was in a file, placed it on the table and with his index finger moved it closer to Ethan as he spoke, "Does anything in that picture look familiar to you?"

Ethan picked the picture up and looked at it a few seconds as he responded, "That's my Bentley right there, you can see my company logo imprinted on the rear windshield of the vehicle." He pointed at the windshield of the car turning the picture in David's and Andrew's direction.

David moved closer to the table as he collected the picture from Ethan, "I reckon you see that man enter your Bentley, that's Igor Krishikov. Sir I ask you again, what are your involvements with Igor Krishikov?"

Ethan looked at David, "Is this the point where you tell me my rights and I ask for my lawyer?"

David smiled as did Andrew, "I really hoped it never got to that point. Holding out with law enforcement wouldn't be the best publicity for a man like you."

Ethan relaxed on his chair as he collected the picture. He looked at the picture and also at David and Andrew as he said, "I don't know your Igor but one thing I know is how my vehicles move and I can give you details of who took a Bentley from me in recent times, but if I do that for you, you have to promise to do one thing for me?"

Andrew replied, "What might that be?"

Ethan continued, "Take my name and my company's name from whatever outcome your investigation gets. You promise me that and I'll grant you access to my files immediately." David looked at Andrew for a few seconds as both agreed to the terms. Ethan unlocked his computer and ran through a few files. He raised his head up as he looked at them both, "It seems there has been just one person who rented a Bentley from me in a while. Andriy Romanov." He turned the monitor of his desktop towards David and Roger as they looked over the records.

"Romanov, the Russian billionaire? What involvement would he have in all of this? This just got really complicating," Andrew replied as he sat down, taking his focus away from the screen.

Ethan responded, "Being a law abiding as myself, if there is anything I can help you with, I'd be more than willing."

David stood up, signalled Andrew. Both appreciated Ethan for his support as they took their leave. They got into the car and drove off. "We have to visit Romanov, I'm not saying he's involved or anything but being Russian makes him the biggest target at the moment."

Driving on the expressway to Romanov's, a white van drove in front of David as did three other off-road trucks. In front of him, a white van, memories flashed through his mind, he didn't know when he shouted out loud, "What is it with people and trying to kill me with white trucks."

Andrew laughed, "You seem pretty sure they are out here to kill you."

"What else does it look like they are trying to do, take us out to dinner? We are in serious trouble mate. Call Roger or Sarah, or HQ, request back up and you might want to strap yourself in properly, it's going to get pretty rough from here on out." Andrew fastened his seatbelt with haste as David stepped on the clutch, twisting the gear stick in a sudden move to surprise the cars that surrounded them, he stepped on the gas pedal as his Peugeot 207 picked up speed, suddenly jolting forward beyond the van, he had the element of surprise as he continued to throttle ferociously to avoid being caught in between the three cars that pursued him. The M25 road was a little quiet on the day as he continued to manoeuvre through what was left of traffic. The pursuers picked up their pace as well as he could hear the engine sound of the truck as it pierced through the winds to his side or even in front of him. It was no day to play nice as David knew that this was an attempt on his life and a move to foil their operations. David knew he had to avoid them using whatever tactics he could come up with.

As he drove through M25, he could see from his side mirrors that they had rifles and were considering shooting at them, he had to exit the open expressway and get into a more busy area where shooting them would be harder but it would mean hitting innocent passers-by, he screamed at Andrew who held tightly to his seat, not wanting to make any costly move, "Why aren't you making that call already?"

Andrew had forgotten what he was asked to do as he quickly reached for his phone in his pocket. He dialled, Roger picked up the phone, and explained their position, "Hey Andrew, we are going to need your help mate, we are under attack at Mark and Laura's, where are you? We need back up ASAP."

Andrew responded, "ASAP? We need your back up, we are currently at the M25 expressway, we have multiple pursuers behind us, shaking them off has been rather unsuccessful." He could hear the sounds of gunshots over the phone as Roger barely had time to respond. He dropped the call as he made attempts to call metropolitan police, as he started to dial, gunshots followed, hitting the rear windshield and all parts of David's car.

"Take positions mate, I'm going to make a sudden right soon, exiting the M25 into Junction 3." Before Andrew could prepare himself, David made a quick right, running the back of the car into the concrete that formed the protective barricades of the road, avoiding just by the whiskers, cars that made the same right turn into Junction 3. In one turn, he had exited the expressway and was headed towards southeast London.

His thoughts could barely remain in place as he wondered what he was on to that was causing this chase. It was quiet as he felt he had outsmarted his pursuers, he didn't stop however as he made attempts to completely avoid them, he tried to drive away but his efforts were futile, he looked into his rear-view mirror and just at the horizon, he could see the two vans covering grounds just to get to him, he stepped on his gas pedal yet again, making a sudden surge forward as he tried to make one last attempt to avoid his pursuers. The pursuers had gain ground on him, they still had the guns at the ready, then he realized there was a quiet road just around the Maidstone channel that he could follow that would reduce civilian casualties and give him another head start on them, he made his way through the cars that stood bamboozled at the speeds he was driving at.

He had no intentions of stopping for no one or no reason. He drove as fast as he could, realizing suddenly that Andrew still wasn't making any call, he looked at Andrew to shake him out of his fear, only to see Andrew holding on to the side of his neck, blood sipping out around his hand and his mouth. Stunned, he thought about stopping the car but that would mean sudden death for them both. Andrew could barely say a word as he held firmly to his injury applying whatever pressure he could as his strength was starting to fade.

He tried to talk but anytime he opened his mouth, blood would hush out in a stream, leaving David confused and hurt as he shouted at him, "Stop talking mate, I'm going to avoid them soon and take you to a hospital, I promised I'd keep you safe, you will be fine, just hang in there with me." He could see Andrew smile a little and he feared the smile. "Was he giving up? Why would he die right now? They were close to the tail end of the case, it is for that sole reason that they are being pursued." He shouted at Andrew who wasn't responding anymore. Holding on to his injury, Andrew thought of limitless possibilities that could have been, seeing out his days in Maldives or Fiji or Hawaii like he always wished would remain a dream, he could no longer be out there saving Britain as this was his end. He had no qualms with it as he had accepted his fate. He had let go of his will to survive as he smiled peacefully until the darkness that is death came over him.

David looked at his friend as he died with a smile, he picked up the phone from Andrew as he dialled metropolitan police, just as the call was picked up, the car behind him bumped into him dropping the phone on the floor. He couldn't pick it up as he had to stay focused on the road. The gunshots resumed as the officer on the other end of the phone could tell that something was wrong. David heard the voice on the other end of the call, but he had not the focus to respond coherently. He screamed through the whole situation, "Under attack, officer down, we need back up, and no, I can't tell you where I am because I'm not sure, I need you to track this call and offer whatever assistance you can as quickly as you can else I'll be dead too soon." He left the call active to allow them to track the call as he made attempts to avoid being killed. David had no intentions of dying before he found out who killed his wife and created a link between his wife's killer and ISIS. As he drove, the sight of his long-time friend Andrew lying lifeless beside him was more than enough reason to survive.

Driving through the suburb, there was a great chance of running into passers-by as David tried to remain focused on the road, driving at top speed, he had managed to stay a step ahead of his pursuers the whole time. As he sped, his phone rang again, he looked down at it, taking his eyes off the road for a few seconds as he saw Rogers call on the phone. Raising his head up, all he could see in front of him was a truck parked just in front waiting for the traffic light to turn green, he had no time to completely avoid it as he turned his steering wheel as hard as he could skewing his car off balance as it turned over, heading straight for a nearby building, the car was upside down as the top made a screeching sound on the road, David could do nothing but hold on firmly to his steering wheel as he hoped for the best. The car continued off course for a few minutes stopping just before it made contact with the house in front of it. The accidents attracted passers-by from all corners of the suburb.

Nearby members of the metropolitan police, who patrolled the area rushed to the scene as his pursuers could not come so close, the driver of the white truck seeing the crowd said to the other guy sitting by him, "There's no way he would have made it out of that accident." They drove away. David laid there unconscious as his phone continued ringing. In the dark, he could see Carla and Kim and now Andrew standing far away. He called them but they couldn't hear him, he tried to pursue after them, but he couldn't move, he felt hands in their numbers grab a hold of him as struggled to free himself, but his efforts proved futile as the hands pulled him through the shopping mall door with bright light on the other side. He struggled to open his eyes as he saw a lot of people standing around him, he could hear the sounds of voices calling for an ambulance as he jumped up to see if Andrew was okay.

The coppers pulled their guns on him as the people dispersed in a hurry, worried he'd react, David raised his hands up as he tried to calm them down, "Put down your weapons lads, I'm law enforcement. I'm not going to harm anyone. The other man in the car, how is he? Where is he?"

The copper looked at Andrew's body laying a few meters away from David's car, "He's dead but I'm sure you knew that already." His gun still pointing straight at David whose countenance changed the moment he realized that Andrew really was dead.

David shouted, "My phone, who has it?"

The copper replied immediately, "I do but I need you to come with me, we can talk this over at the precinct and if really you didn't kill him, you'd be out in no time."

David let out a half-hearted smile, "You don't understand what is going on lad, it's bigger than you, it's bigger than me, I need my phone, my car and I'll be out of here."

The officer responded, "You know I can't allow that; I need to be sure you didn't kill your friend here."

As they argued, his phone rang, David told him, "I need to get that mate, a lot is riding on me taking that call, your life, their lives and all of Britain needs me to answer that call."

The officer looked at the call, "I would have taken that a lot serious if the Prime Minister was the one calling but it's just a guy named Roger, how important could it be you talking to Roger? For all I know, Roger could be your accomplice in this murder and maybe even numerous other crimes."

David laughed as he replied, "I like that you are doing your job but you are really starting to piss me off. Pick it up if you doubt me."

The officer hesitated but he summoned the courage to pick up the call, he kept quiet as he waited for Roger to start the conversation which Roger did eventually, "What is going on with you David, we just have to fend off a handful of terrorists, what is the update on your end?"

Out of shock, the copper walked towards David, "You might be telling the truth."

He handed the phone over to David who responded reluctantly, "We got hit and pretty hard too, Andrew didn't make it out, he got hit, I barely made it out myself. You lot head on to Romanov's estate, he has affinity with ISIS and I think he found out somehow that we are on to him and I think I know how he found out, I'm a little off track but I'll meet you there as fast as I can, call for backup because I think it's not going to be easy. They seem really prepared to knock us off."

Roger, shocked to hear of the death of Andrew, remained quiet for a while before he responded, "I hope your fine mate?"

David sighed as he replied, "I am fine, I'll meet you there ASAP. Just be safe yourself, I'm not going to lose anyone else."

CHAPTER TWENTY-SEVEN: CHALLENGE

After David had finished talking to Roger, he looked at the copper and his partner as they remained quiet waiting for him to speak up first, when they realized he wasn't saying anything, they said, "How can we help you sir?"

David smiled as he responded, "Welcome on board, I need you to request backup to Romanov's estate, as many as the metropolitan police can muster. I need your car as well and you both. What is your names lad?"

The copper stuttered, "My name's Jake sir and my partner's Harry, we are glad to be of service sir."

David picked up his phone as he made a call to GCHQ's director, who picked up almost as quickly as the phone rang, "What do you have for me David?"

David responded just as quickly, "We have reasons to believe that whoever killed my wife is involved with ISIS somehow and we have created a link between Carla's murderer and Russian Billionaire Andriy Romanov. We were headed there for questions when we were attacked, Roger, Sarah and Josh were also attacked simultaneously."

The director, shocked to his marrow, asked, "I hope your fine mate?"

David replied, "I wish I could say it is sir, we lost Andrew, he was shot during the car chase but I am fine and I'm heading for Romanov's estate. If he isn't involved, he'd better have a really good explanation as to why a car he rented was used to kill Carla as why we were suddenly attacked the moment, we tied him to the case. I might be wrong, but I feel strongly that he has something to do with ISIS. I need a favour though sir."

The director responded, his voice had lost its power hearing of Andrew's death, "Anything you want, just say it."

David replied, "I need you to trust my instincts and send back up to Romanov's estate, I don't know why but I think there'd be resistance and pull up information about Romanov, I need to know where he's at right now, I need updates about him every few seconds." The director agreed as the two coppers that sat with David remained dumbfounded. David looked at them, "You might be in over your head here lads, but you'll do great, just remain calm and don't try to be heroes and you'll be fine." David drove through the streets of southeast London as he headed for Romanov's estate.

He pressed the pedal of the car till he was sure it couldn't be pressed further, the coppers held unto the car for dear life as David made no attempt to slow down, cutting through traffic like he was being pursued, driving in a cop car, he had no reason to slow down, he had in his heart, revenge and the desire to protect his beloved country. A few minutes to the estate, he got a call from Roger, "It's an angry crowd David, we were met with serious resistance, they knew we were coming and are well prepared to take us on, we are taking massive damage already, and we need more back up ASAP."

David replied, "I have already made that request, just hold on a little, they will be there in a short time. What of Igor or Romanov or Mark or Laura?"

Roger replied as David could hear clearly the gunshots from the phone, "We haven't made it in, I cannot tell you who is in there or not, all I can say for now is that I think there's something in there that they are trying to protect, they have a shopping mall army here." Heading to the Romanov estate from southeast London, he took a different route than everybody else, on his way, a convoy of vehicles passed him, heading in the opposite direction. He couldn't explain it but he felt in his gut that that was Romanov.

He thought about it for a while that it could be Romanov and after a few seconds, he pressed his brakes as he pulled up his hand brakes, making a U-turn on the expressway as he stepped on the gas pedal, going after the very convoy that just passed. Jake asked, "Shouldn't we be headed for Romanov's estate sir?"

David replied, "I think that Romanov just drove pass us, he's attempting to escape." David pursued after the convoy as best he could try not to get too close to be noticed but also not to stay too far so he wouldn't miss them. In a short while, they had arrived at a private airstrip. He took cover, looking from a safe spot, he saw Mark and Laura come down from an Escalade as did Igor Krishikov, Romanov was the last to come down from another vehicle, this time a dodge as they had a private jet wait for them at the strip.

There weren't much in terms of guards but a handful, and David was determined not to let them escape. Sneaking through the airstrip, David headed for the private jet. Romanov and Igor stood anxiously waiting for it to get to where they were with Mark and Laura standing, waiting as well. David, hiding behind the hanger alongside Jake and Harry, watched patiently as Jake made the call for backup. David brought out his 9mm, he had just two rounds on him, and he had lost some during the accident. He sneaked out, slowly but as he walked, just by a whisker, a bullet passed him hitting his bicep, he screamed in pain as it alerted Igor and Romanov who took cover in the hanger. David managed, holding his hand to pull himself into a covered corner as what was left of Romanov's guards heard his screams turned towards him and started shooting at him.

Not sure where he was shot from, David stayed hidden, he had dropped his phone where he was shot and couldn't go out for it, and he had his 9mm in his hand as he managed to tie his left to stop the bleeding. He heard someone calling his name as the shooting subsided, "I reckon it's your David Scarlet, I hope you don't hate me too much about what happened to your beloved wife, it's not something against you, it's just something I had to do, I must say that you don't have the right to be angry at me. You left me a souvenir at Zhovkva, my brother, my only reason for being alive, you took him from me. Like a seasoned assassin, you slit his throat, not giving him a fair trial like you law enforcement always claim to do. But you need not worry, I didn't kill Carla for revenge, I did for a reason you might never find out. Kill him."

David tried to buy time not sure if anyone was coming for him, he knew he had Jake and Harry with him, but he couldn't really put his life in the hands of two rookies, he replied, "If it's any consolation, I didn't kill your brother, you could say you did, he took his own life to cover up your agenda, it was pretty disheartening seeing a young man with so much promise end his life to protect his brother whom he loves, adores and looks up to. You failed him, the same way you are working hard to fail your own country. Yes, I know you are English, picked up some information from young Lucas that helped us know who you are. You might be Russian by descent, but you have lived your entire life in Britain, what did they offer you, money, power?"

"You don't know anything about me, David, I always wanted to meet you and you and I could be friends in a different life, I came to Britain as a kid, my brother was born here, my family came here with a purpose, my father couldn't achieve it but I have, I have Britain in my hand, I could do as I please and get away with it. Even if I die right now, it doesn't stop this movement, there'll be more like me in my place. You on the other hand will die here and that will be the last of David Scarlet. I know you just as much as you know me, your exploits in Saudi Arabia and my home country. I'll kill you here and take the credit." He laughed as David raised his head over the crate he was hiding, he was outnumbered and cornered. He was going to die; he knew that but he wasn't going down without a fight.

David replied to Igor, "What has Mark and Laura got to do with this? Let them go so they can mourn their daughter."

Igor laughed out loud before he continued talking, "You don't know as much as you claim to know, let me fill you in on something, Carla was the first case of a Declon 5 death in London and lots more will follow and it wasn't I who injected your beloved wife with the fatal agent, you want to tell him Mark or should I?"

Mark walked out with a berretta in his hand pointing towards David, he had an expression on his face that confused David who wasn't sure if he was remorseful or not, he told David, "I did it, I killed Carla. I did you a favour if you bother to want to see it that way, she wasn't your beloved wife, and she was dangerous to you as she was to me so I had to put an end to her."

David was confused, not sure what to say or do, Igor continued speaking, "Let me simplify that for you, Carla never loved you, she had always used you as a means to an end and she was going to dispose of you eventually. She was one of ours before she got corrupted and we had to put her out of commission."

David was getting pissed as he responded, "If you are not going to be straightforward with what happened with my wife, I suggest you take her name out your filthy mouth. Whatever she must have done, killing the unborn child? You are a joke of a man and I will kill you here."

"Making such bold claims from someone who is alive just because I haven't given the go ahead? You are even more than I heard you are. Kill him lads and make it really painful."

Just as Igor made the statement, he turned back to head for the private jet when Jake came out holding Romanov hostage. "Let him go or I kill him," Jake threatened Igor, who didn't seem the least bit concerned.

Igor laughed as he replied, "You think I care about him? Shoot him, see if I care. You know what lads, kill the childcopper first, make David watch and then kill David afterwards, it'll hurt more that way."

David shouted, "Don't do that, he is just a kid, he doesn't have to die, at least not today, not on my watch, I beg you."

Igor laughed as he turned towards David, "It shouldn't bother you that one childwill die today, a lot will die beginning tomorrow only if you don't stop what's coming."

Romanov interrupted Igor as he spoke, "Igor you bastard! Kill me? After all I've done for you? Without me you wouldn't be where you are right now, you owe me and this is how you pay me?"

Igor looked at him, "I owe you nothing."

He walked towards the jet, as did Mark and Laura, the rest of the men, holding rifles in their hands were about to open fire when an explosion rocked one of the hangers in the strip. Shockwaves followed as everyone was thrown to the floor, Jake just like everyone fell on the ground but being farthest from the explosion was to his advantage as he made away with Romanov heading for safety.

When David heard the explosion, he knew his stalling had worked out, an explosion entry as Josh always called it was his signature entrance, David knew his teammates had arrived. He sneaked out heading for the jet to intercept Igor, Mark and Laura. The rest of the terrorists got up after the explosion, heading straight for Josh, Roger and Sarah and the handful of coppers that had made their way to the airstrip. Gunshots filled the air as the men exchanged fire, David took advantage of the commotion. Igor was already entering the jet when David shot at him, multiple times but none making contact. He rushed into the jet but Laura wasn't so lucky as one of the bullets had hit her on the lower abdomen. Mark pulled her into the jet anyway as David ran towards it which was starting to move. David was resilient not willing to give up, he pursued on foot, trying to stop it but to his surprise, the jet started to slope down. He wasn't sure but he had to take advantage of it, he rushed over and forced the door open as he heard a solitary gunshot, amidst the recurring gun fire, this particular gunshot sent chills down his spine as he boarded the jet, slowly not wanting to be seen. He saw Laura lying on the floor in a pool of blood, but Mark was nowhere in sight. He sneaked in, he walked to Laura, checked her pulse as she still had a pulse, just as he was about to walk away from her, Mark jumped him, hitting him behind as he fell to the floor.

Mark mounted him, landing blow after blow, he was slow to defend himself as all that was in his mind was all the memories they had shared together. The jet started to move yet again as he realized he had to get off the jet. Mark threw a right hand at his face but he moved his head just slightly to the left allowing his hand to make contact with the floor of the jet as Mark held on to his hurt knuckle, trying to brace himself for another when David gave him an uppercut on his chin as he spit blood allowing David the chance to land blow after blow, sending Mark to the floor. David stood up, kicking him over and over again on the stomach, mounting him. David landed blow after blow until Mark was unconscious, he picked his 9mm as he headed for the cockpit, the jet still on the runway was picking up speed.

David jumped into the cockpit gun first but was grabbed by Igor, the pair struggling to get hold of the gun. Amidst the struggle for the gun, the jet had taken off, nose up, it was heading for the open skies. David shot the gun, this time hitting the sole pilot on his neck as the air bound jet began to nosedive, it hadn't gone far into the air so with the momentum that it had lifted, it was heading down, Igor made his way from the cockpit, running towards the end of the jet. David looked around the cockpit and saw Harry on the floor, a single gunshot wound on his chest. He knew nothing about flying planes as he dashed towards the end of the plane.

The collision happened so fast that in no time, a thunderous sound was heard across the airstrip as the jet made contact with the floor, the cockpit, breaking away from the rest of the plane as David ran to the back. In a few minutes, the jet was on the floor, split in two. David opened his eyelids as he looked around for Igor. He didn't see Igor in the wreckage but as he stood up, he saw Laura, holding her abdomen in pain as Mark laid unconscious by her side. He looked around as he saw Igor running away from the scene, he followed him, holding his head as he bled from his head, the impact of the crash. He followed David who had made his way into a hanger to hide. Just as he entered the hanger, Igor hit him with a piece of wood, but he was able to avert the full force, receiving a hit just in his lower back as he fell to the ground, a sharp pain shooting up his spine as he felt his body spasm. For the first time in a long time, his nervous disorder came back. He felt his muscles occasionally vibrate as he struggled to pick himself up, Igor wouldn't allow him as he continued hitting him over and over, David managed to cover his head avoiding damage to his head, but he could hardly keep up as the swings came quickly after each other. He was starting to lose consciousness as he knew he had failed in his desire for revenge, he came in for revenge, but he was the one who'd get killed, his grip all over his head was starting to fade, his hands opening up when he heard a solitary gunshot. Whoever was shot he didn't know but the rampage on his face had stopped.

He struggled to raise his head to see who had stopped it and he saw Sarah standing with a handgun in her hand and blood dripping from Igor's neck as he fell back on his head and darkness overcame him. He woke up a while after with the metropolitan police rounding up what was left of the terrorists. It was a victory for London but at what cost? A lot of coppers had lost their lives. His eyes swollen and his injuries, he came down from the bed he was lying, looked around, he saw Jake standing over Harry's body, he walked over to the young copper, "I told you both not to be heroes, but you didn't listen." Jake was going to explain but tears rolled down his cheeks as he was unable to speak. David continued, "I was wrong, you deciding to be heroes has saved our country, Harry, your friend, and your partner was the bravest man I've ever met. His sacrifice saved us all." He saluted at Jake as he responded, still with tears rolling down his cheeks, and David hugged the young cop as he saluted also at Harry's body lying on the bed.

As David paid his last respects to Harry, Roger, Josh and Sarah approached him, he turned clutching his right ribs as he felt the pain the most right there, Roger still not looking easy said to him, "We found the Declon 5 files, but we still have a problem. We don't know if it has been used or not."

David slowly collected the files as he replied, "It hasn't been, but it will be if we don't find out where and how, Igor mentioned it."

Sarah joined in, "Britain is a huge country, how are we supposed to know where it'd be used?"

David limped towards the coppers' cars, "I know how. I just need you to be ready to go at any time. I can barely move as it is." He walked straight for the car which had Romanov and Mark.

Getting there, he ordered the officer to bring them out which he did, standing in front of him in handcuffs, Mark kept his head down unable to even look at David with Romanov trying his hardest to broker a deal for a release. David slowly approached Mark as did Roger, Sarah and Josh as he said to Mark, "I have loved and respected you my entire life only for you to throw that away, I don't know who you are, but I can tell you are not proud of your actions so far. Do your conscience a favour and just tell us your plans. Is it a dirty bomb or are you going to put the Declon 5 in the water? Think of Carla and your grandchild, how would they feel if you refuse to help us."

Mark was in tears, "I didn't mean to kill so many innocent people, I just came for the files and when I got it, I wanted to leave but Igor had other ideas."

David placed his hand on Mark's shoulders, "We can end this, just tell us how."

Mark, still crying, started talking as Romanov stood there dumbfounded, "Right about now, a really large amount of the Declon 5 is mixed with the water supply at Thames water, affinity water and essence and Suffolk water. The plan is to supply it to households and have them drink it, plunging Britain into chaos, beginning with London, he was going to spread his wings to all the reaches of Europe, he had forgotten why we came to London in the first place."

David signalled to Roger who left immediately with Sarah and Josh as David went straight to Mark, "Tell me, what Carla did to deserve death and where Kim is?"

Mark let his back slide off the car as he fell to the floor, "I have to tell you, Carla, Igor, Laura and I are agents sent from Moscow to attend to some issues. I don't know what Igor did or say but our mission was changed to retrieving the Declon 5 files and the agent, which he did with my help. He demanded Carla killed when he found out, Carla was doubling for British intelligence. I didn't want to but he made me do it, it was that or I am killed."

David cut in, "You mean to say Carla was a British spy also working for Russia?" Mark nodded his head. David shook his head, not sure if to believe it or not, he turned his back as he walked away, but stopped and turned, "What did you do to Kim?"

Mark tried to look at David as he replied, "She's fine, no harm has been done to her, and we dropped her off at the orphanage and told them to contact you in seventy-two hours if we didn't come back for her. I promise you; she is fine."

David walked away from Mark as the officer took him and Romanov into the police car and drove away. David had one agenda in his mind, to get back his baby girl. He left in the car he had gotten there with. Driving straight for the orphanage, his phone rang, it was the director of the GCHQ on the phone, excitedly, he said to David, "Congratulations on your resounding success, the people of London and indeed Britain can rest easy today thanks to the efforts of you and your team—"

"How long did you know Carla was a spy and was it you who gave her the job as an English spy?" The director hesitated in his response and just as he was about to speak, David cut him short yet again, "Carla's death is on you, involving her in something that is way bigger than her. I want no part of your celebrations. Sarah and Roger will return to GCHQ and you will honour them, you will give Andrew a proper hero's burial and most importantly, you will forget I exist. Don't look for me because you won't find me." He got to the orphanage where he found Kim, sitting on the front porch waiting for him. Seeing him, she ran to him as she hugged him tight, he lifted her up in the air as he kissed her gently on the cheeks as the pair walked towards his car.

His phone rang, it was Roger who had called to let him know that they had secured the factories and ensured the Declon 5 wasn't going to be spread into London, David replied calmly, "It's been a pleasure working with you and the others Roger but from here on out, it's about you guys, I'm about to fade in the shadows and hope out of respect, I'm left there, send the message to Sarah and Josh. In as much as I'd like to see you all some other time, I hope we do that not on work terms." He dropped the call as he walked away with Kim walking besides him.

He had one call to make, it was to the Prime Minister who picked up immediately, "David, my old mate, I just heard of the success you score over ISIS. I'm happy for you, I hope to see you back at work as soon as possible yeah. So, we can continue from where we left off with chess," he laughed out loud as he waited for David's response.

David replied, "I'd have loved to play chess with you again sir, but I don't think it'd be possible. I'm taking time off and I hope you don't come looking for me. I'm spending whatever time left I have with Kim. I have but one thing to say, stay ready, I don't think this is the last we'll see of ISIS. Keep my team in good shape and they'll be there when next you need them." The Prime Minister had no words as David bade him farewell, threw the phone in a nearby Skip as he drove into the sunset with Kim by his side.

Printed in Poland
by Amazon Fulfillment
Poland Sp. z o.o., Wrocław
15 December 2022

b0fc06a2-0acf-4ae5-95fd-6f123e3f8767R01